10534432

AMOK

AND OTHER STORIES

STEFAN ZWEIG

AMOK

AND OTHER STORIES

Translated from the German by
Anthea Bell

PUSHKIN PRESS
LONDON

For Federico, in memory of Matteo

Original texts © Williams Verlag A G Zurich

Amok
First published in German as
Amok in 1922

The Star above the Forest
First published in German as
Der Stern über dem Walde in 1904

Leporella
First published in German as
Leporella in 1954

Incident on Lake Geneva
This revised text first published in German as
Episode am Genfer See in 1936

English translation © Anthea Bell

First published in 2006 by
Pushkin Press
12 Chester Terrace
London N1 4ND

Reprinted 2007
Reprinted 2010

ISBN 978 1 901285 66 6

All rights reserved. No part of this publication may be reproduced,
stored in a retrieval system or transmitted in any form or by any
means, electronic, mechanical, photocopying, recording or
otherwise, without prior permission in writing from
Pushkin Press

Cover: *Sleeve of the Dervish* 17th C Safavid tile
Courtesy of Simon Ray London

Frontispiece: Portrait of Stefan Zweig
© Roger-Viollet Rex Features

Set in 10 on 12 Baskerville Monotype
and printed on Munken Premium White 90gsm
by TJ International Ltd Padstow Cornwall

www.pushkinpress.com

CONTENTS

AMOK

IN MARCH 1912 A STRANGE ACCIDENT occurred in Naples harbour during the unloading of a large ocean-going liner which was reported at length by the newspapers, although in extremely fanciful terms. Although I was a passenger on the *Oceania*, I did not myself witness this strange incident— nor did any of the others—since it happened while coal was being taken on board and cargo unloaded, and to escape the noise we had all gone ashore to pass the time in coffee- houses or theatres. It is my personal opinion however, that a number of conjectures which I did not voice publicly at the time provide the true explanation of that sensational event, and I think that, at a distance of some years, I may now be permitted to give an account of a conversation I had in con- fidence immediately before the curious episode.

When I went to the Calcutta shipping agency trying to book a passage on the *Oceania* for my voyage home to Europe, the clerk apologetically shrugged his shoulders. He didn't know if it would be possible for him to get me a cabin, he said; at this time of year, with the rainy season imminent, the ship was likely to be fully booked all the way from Australia, and he would have to wait for a telegram from Singapore. Next day, I was glad to hear, he told me that yes, he could still reserve me a cabin, although not a particularly comfortable one; it would be below deck and amidships. As I was impatient to get home I did not hesitate for long, but took it.

The clerk had not misinformed me. The ship was over-crowded and my cabin a poor one: a cramped little rectangle of a place near the engine room, lit only dimly through a circular porthole. The thick, curdled air smelled greasy and musty, and I could not for a moment escape the electric ventilator fan that hummed as it circled overhead like a steel bat gone mad. Down below the engines clattered and groaned like a breathless coal-heaver constantly climbing the same flight of stairs, up above I heard the tramp of footsteps pacing the promenade deck the whole time. As soon as I had stowed my luggage away amidst the dingy girders in my stuffy tomb, I then went back on deck to get away from the place, and as I came up from the depths I drank in the soft, sweet wind blowing off the land as if it were ambrosia.

But the atmosphere of the promenade deck was crowded and restless too, full of people chattering incessantly, hurrying up and down with the uneasy nervousness of those forced to be inactive in a confined space. The arch flirtatiousness of the women, the constant pacing up and down on the bottleneck of the deck as flocks of passengers surged past the deckchairs, always meeting the same faces again, were actually painful to me. I had seen a new world, I had taken in turbulent, confused images that raced wildly through my mind. Now I wanted leisure to think, to analyse and organise them, make sense of all that had impressed itself on my eyes, but there wasn't a moment of rest and peace to be had here on the crowded deck. The lines of a book I was trying to read blurred as the fleeting shadows of the chattering passengers moved by. It was impossible to be alone with myself on the unshaded, busy thoroughfare of the deck of this ship.

I tried for three days; resigned to my lot, I watched the passengers and the sea. But the sea was always the same, blue and empty, and only at sunset was it abruptly flooded with every imaginable colour. As for the passengers, after seventy-two hours I knew them all by heart. Every face was tediously familiar, the women's shrill laughter no longer irritated me, even the loud voices of two Dutch officers quarrelling nearby were not such a source of annoyance any more. There was nothing for it but to escape the deck, although my cabin was hot and stuffy, and in the saloon English girls kept playing waltzes badly on the piano, staccato-fashion. Finally I decided to turn the day's normal timetable upside down, and in the afternoon, having anaesthetized myself with a few glasses of beer, I went to my cabin to sleep through the evening with its dinner and dancing.

When I woke it was dark and oppressive in the little coffin of my cabin. I had switched off the ventilator, so the air around my temples felt greasy and humid. My senses were bemused, and it took me some minutes to remember my surroundings and wonder what the time was. It must have been after midnight, anyway, for I could not hear music or those restless footsteps pacing overhead. Only the engine, the breathing heart of the leviathan, throbbed as it thrust the body of the ship on into the unseen.

I made my way up to the deck. It was deserted. And as I looked above the steam from the funnel and the ghostly gleam of the spars, a magical brightness suddenly met my eyes. The sky was radiant, dark behind the white stars wheeling through it and yet radiant, as if a velvet curtain up there veiled a great light, and the twinkling stars were merely gaps and cracks through which that indescribable brightness shone. I had never before seen the sky as I saw it that night, glowing with such radiance, hard and steely blue, and yet light came sparkling, dripping, pouring, gushing down, falling from the moon and stars as if burning in some mysterious inner space. The white-painted outlines of the ship stood out bright against the velvety dark sea in the moonlight, while all the detailed contours of the ropes and the yards dissolved in that flowing brilliance; the lights on the masts seemed to hang in space, with the round eye of the lookout post above them, earthly yellow stars amidst the shining stars of the sky.

And right above my head stood the magical constellation of the Southern Cross, hammered into the invisible void with shining diamond nails and seeming to hover, although only the ship was really moving, quivering slightly as it made its way up and down with heaving breast, up and down, a gigantic swimmer passing through the dark waves. I stood there looking up; I felt as if I were bathed by warm water falling from above, except that it was light washing over my hands, mild, white light pouring around my shoulders, my head, and seeming to permeate me entirely, for all at once everything sombre about me was brightly lit. I breathed freely, purely, and full of sudden delight I felt the air on my lips like a clear drink. It was soft, effervescent air carrying on it the aroma of fruits, the scent of distant islands, and making me feel slightly drunk. Now, for the first time since I had set foot on the ship's planks, I knew the blessed joy of reverie, and the other more sensual pleasure of abandoning my body, woman-like, to the softness surrounding me. I wanted to lie down and look up at the white hieroglyphs in the sky. But the loungers and deckchairs had been cleared away, and there was nowhere for me to rest and dream on the deserted promenade deck.

So I made my way on, gradually approaching the bows of the ship, dazzled by the light that seemed to be shining more and more intensely on everything around me. It almost hurt, that bright, glaring, burning starlight, and I wanted to find a place to lie on a mat in deep shade, feeling the glow not on me but only above me, reflected in the ship's gear around me as one sees a landscape from a darkened room. At last, stumbling over cables and past iron hoists, I reached the ship's side and looked down over the keel to see the bows moving on into the blackness, while molten moonlight sprayed up, foaming, on both sides of their path. The ship kept rising and falling, rising and falling in the flowing dark, cutting through the black water as a plough cuts through soil, and in that sparkling interplay I felt all the torment of the conquered element and all the pleasures of earthly power. As I watched I lost all sense of time. Did I stand there for an hour, or was it only minutes? The vast cradle of the ship moving up and down rocked me away from time, and I felt only a pleasant weariness coming over me, a sensuous feeling. I wanted to sleep, to dream, yet I did not wish to leave this magic and go back down into my coffin. I instinctively felt around with my foot and found a coil of ropes. I sat down on it with my eyes closed yet not fully darkened, for above them, above me, that silver glow streamed on. Below me I felt the water rushing quietly on, above me the white torrent flowed by with inaudible resonance. And gradually the rushing sound passed into my blood; I was no longer conscious of myself, I didn't know if I heard my own breathing or the distant, throbbing heart of the ship, I myself was streaming, pouring away in the never-resting midnight world as it raced past.

A dry, harsh cough quite close to me made me jump. I came out of my half-intoxicated reverie with a start. My eyes, which even through closed lids had been dazzled by the white brightness, now searched around: quite close, and opposite me in the shadow of the ship's side, something glinted like light reflected off a pair of glasses, and now I saw the concentrated and circular glow of a lighted pipe. As I sat down, looking only below at the foaming bows as they cut through the waves or up at the Southern Cross, I had obviously failed to notice my neighbour, who must have been sitting here perfectly still all the time. Instinctively, my reactions still slow, I said in German, "Oh, I do apologise!" "Don't mention it," replied the voice from the darkness, in the same language.

I can't say how strange and eerie it was to be sitting next to someone like that in the dark, very close to a man I couldn't see. I felt as if he were staring at me just as I was staring at him, but the flowing, shimmering white light above us was so intense that neither of us could see more of the other than his outline in the shadows. And I thought I could hear his breathing and the faint hissing sound as he drew on his pipe, but that was all.

The silence was unbearable. I wanted to move away, but that seemed too brusque, too sudden. In my embarrassment I took out a cigarette. The match spluttered, and for a second its light flickered over the narrow space where we were sitting. I saw a stranger's face behind the lenses of his glasses, a face I had never seen on board at any meal or on the promenade deck, and whether the sudden flame hurt the man's eyes, or whether it was just an illusion, his face suddenly seemed dreadfully distorted, dark and goblin-like. But before I could make out any details, darkness swallowed up the fleetingly illuminated features again, and I saw only the outline of a figure darkly imprinted on the darkness, and sometimes the circular, fiery ring of the bowl of his pipe hovering in space. Neither of us spoke, and our silence was as sultry and oppressive as the tropical air itself.

Finally I could stand it no longer. I stood up and said a civil, "Goodnight."

"Goodnight," came the reply from the darkness, in a hoarse, harsh, rusty voice.

I stumbled forward with some difficulty, over hawsers and past some posts. Then I heard footsteps behind me, hasty and uncertain. It was my companion of a moment ago. I instinctively stopped. He did not come right up to me, and through the darkness I sensed something like anxiety and awkwardness in his gait.

"Forgive me," he said quickly "if I ask you a favour. I … I … " he stammered, for a moment too embarrassed to go on at once. "I … I have private … very private reasons for staying out of sight … a bereavement ... I prefer to avoid company on board. Oh, I didn't mean you, no, no … I'd just like to ask … well, I would be very much obliged if you wouldn't mention seeing me here to anyone on board. There are … are private reasons, I might call them, to keep me from mingling with people just now … yes, well, it would put me in an awkward position if you mentioned that someone … here at night … that I … " And he stopped again. I put an end to his confusion at once by assuring him that I would do as he wished. We shook hands. Then I went back to my cabin and slept a heavy, curiously disturbed sleep, troubled by strange images.

I kept my promise, and told no one on board of my strange meeting, although the temptation to do so was great. For on a sea voyage every little thing becomes an event: a sail on the horizon, a dolphin leaping, a new flirtation, a joke made in passing. And I was full of curiosity to know more about the vessel's unusual passenger. I searched the ship's list for a name that might be his, I scrutinized other people, wondering if they could be somehow related to him; all day I was a prey to nervous impatience, just waiting for evening and wondering if I would meet him again. Odd psychological states have a positively disquieting power over me; I find tracking down the reasons for them deeply intriguing, and the mere presence of unusual characters can kindle a passionate desire in me to know more about them, a desire not much less strong than a woman's wish to acquire some possession. The day seemed long and crumbled tediously away between my fingers. I went to bed early, knowing that my curiosity would wake me at midnight.

Sure enough, I woke at the same time as the night before. The two hands on the illuminated dial of my clock covered one another in a single bright line. I quickly left my sultry cabin and climbed up into the even sultrier night.

The stars were shining as they had shone yesterday, casting a diffuse light over the quivering ship, and the Southern Cross blazed high overhead. It was all just the same as yesterday, where days and nights in the tropics resemble each other more than in our latitudes, but I myself did not feel yesterday's soft, flowing, dreamy sensation of being gently cradled. Something was drawing me on, confusing me, and I knew where it was taking me: to the black hoist by the ship's side, to see if my mysterious acquaintance was sitting immobile there again. I heard the ship's bell striking above me, and it urged me on. Step by step, reluctantly yet fascinated, I followed my instincts. I had not yet reached the prow of the ship when something like a red eye suddenly hovered in front of me: the pipe. So he was there.

I instinctively stepped back and stopped. Next moment I would have left again, but there was movement over there in the dark, something rose, took a couple of steps, and suddenly I heard his voice very close to me, civil and melancholy.

"Forgive me," he said. "You obviously want to sit there again, and I have a feeling that you hesitated when you saw me. Do please sit down, and I'll go away."

19

I made haste to say he was very welcome to stay so far as I was concerned. I had stepped back, I said, only for fear of disturbing him.

"Oh, you won't disturb me," he said, with some bitterness. "Far from it, I'm glad to have company for a change. I haven't spoken a word to anyone for ten days … well, not for years, really, and then it seems so difficult, perhaps because forcing it all back inside myself chokes me. I can't sit in my cabin any more, in that … that coffin, I can't bear it, and I can't bear the company of human beings either because they laugh all day … I can't endure that now, I hear it in my cabin and stop my ears against it. Of course, they don't know that I … well, they don't know that … they don't know it, and what business is it of theirs, after all, they're strangers … "

He stopped again, and then very suddenly and hastily said, "But I don't want to bother you … forgive me for speaking so freely."

He made a bow, and was about to leave, but I urged him to stay. "You're not bothering me in the least. I'm glad to have a few quiet words with someone up here myself … may I offer you a cigarette?"

He took one, and I lit it. Once again his face moved away from the ship's black side, flickering in the light of the match, but now he turned it fully to me: his eyes behind his glasses looking inquiringly into my face, avidly and with demented force. A shudder passed through me. I could feel that this man wanted to speak, had to speak. And I knew that I must help him by saying nothing.

We sat down again. He had a second deckchair there, and offered it to me. Our cigarettes glowed, and from the way that the ring of light traced by his in the darkness shook, I could tell that his hand was trembling. But I kept silent, and so did he. Then, suddenly, he asked in a quiet voice, "Are you very tired?"

"No, not at all."

The voice in the dark hesitated again. "I would like to ask you something … that's to say, I'd like to tell you something. Oh, I know, I know very well how absurd it is to turn to the first man I meet, but … I'm … I'm in a terrible mental condition, I have reached a point where I absolutely must talk to someone, or it will be the end of me … You'll understand that when I … well, if I tell you … I mean, I know you can't help me, but this silence is almost making me ill, and a sick man always looks ridiculous to others … "

Here I interrupted, begging him not to distress himself. He could tell me anything he liked, I said. Naturally I couldn't promise him anything, but to show willingness is a human duty. If you see someone in trouble, I added, of course it is your duty to help …

"Duty … to show willing … a duty to try to … so you too think it is a man's duty … yes, his duty to show himself willing to help."

He repeated it three times. I shuddered at the blunt, grim tone of his repetition. Was the man mad? Was he drunk?

As if I had uttered my suspicions aloud, he suddenly said in quite a different voice, "You may think me mad or drunk. No, I'm not—not yet. Only what you said moved me so … so strangely, because that's exactly what torments me now, wondering if it's a duty … a duty … "

He was beginning to stammer again. He broke off for a moment, pulled himself together, and began again.

"The fact is, I am a doctor of medicine, and in that profession we often come upon such cases, such fateful cases … borderline cases, let's call them, when we don't know whether or not it is our duty … or rather, when there's more than one duty involved, not just to another human being but to ourselves too, to the state, to science … yes, of course, we must help, that's what we are there for … but such maxims are never more than theory. How far should we go with our help? Here are you, a stranger to me, and I'm a stranger to you, and I ask you not to mention seeing me … well, so you don't say anything, you do that duty … and now I ask you to talk to me because my own silence is killing me, and you say you are ready to listen. Good, but that's easy … suppose I were to ask you to take hold of me and throw me overboard, though, your willingness to help would be over. The duty has to end somewhere … it ends where we begin thinking of our own lives, our own responsibilities, it has to end somewhere, it has to end … or perhaps for doctors, of all people, it ought *not* to end? Must a doctor always come to the rescue, be ready to help one and all, just because he has a diploma full of Latin words, must he really throw away his life and water down his own blood if some woman … if someone comes along wanting him to be noble, helpful, good? Yes, duty ends somewhere … it ends where no more can be done, that's where it ends … "

He stopped again, and regained control.

"Forgive me, I know I sound agitated … but I'm not drunk, not yet … although I often am, I freely confess it, in this hellish isolation … bear in mind that for seven years I've lived almost entirely with the local natives and with animals … you forget how to talk calmly. And then if you do open up, everything comes flooding out … but wait … Yes, I know … I was going to ask you, I wanted to tell you about a certain case, wondering whether you think one has a duty to help … just help, with motives as pure as an angel's, or whether … Although I fear it will be a long story. Are you sure you're not tired?"

"No, not in the least."

"Thank you … thank you. Will you have a drink?"

He had been groping in the dark behind him somewhere. There was a clinking sound: two or three, at any rate several bottles stood ranged there. He offered me a glass of whisky, which I sipped briefly, while he drained his glass in a single draught. For a moment there was silence between us. Then the ship's bell struck half-past midnight.

"Well then … I'd like to tell you about a case. Suppose that a doctor in a small town … or right out in the country, a doctor who … a doctor who … " He stopped again, and then suddenly moved his chair closer to mine.

"This is no good. I must tell you everything directly, from the beginning, or you won't understand it … no, I can't put it as a theoretical example, I must tell you the story of my own case. There'll be no shame about it, I will hide nothing … people strip naked in front of me, after all, and show me their scabs, their urine, their excrement

… if someone is to help there can be no beating about the bush, no concealment. So I won't describe the case of some fictional doctor, I will strip myself naked and say that I … I forgot all shame in that filthy isolation, that accursed country that eats the soul and sucks the marrow from a man's loins."

I must have made a movement of some kind, for he interrupted himself.

"Ah, you protest … oh, I understand, you are fascinated by India, by its temples and palm trees, all the romance of a two-month visit. Yes, the tropics are magical when you're travelling through them by rail, road or rickshaw: I felt just the same when I first arrived seven years ago. I had so many dreams, I was going to learn the language and read the sacred texts in the original, I was going to study the diseases, do scientific work, explore the native psyche—as we would put it in European jargon—I was on a mission for humanity and civilisation. Everyone who comes here dreams the same dream. But then a man's strength ebbs away in this invisible hothouse, the fever strikes deep into him—and we all get the fever, however much quinine we take—he becomes listless, indolent, flabby as a jellyfish. As a European, he is cut off from his true nature, so to speak, when he leaves the big cities for some wretched swamp-ridden station. Sooner or later we all succumb to our weaknesses, some drink, others smoke opium, others again brawl and act like brutes—some kind of folly comes over us all. We long for Europe, we dream of walking down a street again some day, sitting among white people in a well-lit room in a solidly built house, we dream of it year after year, and if a time does come when we could go on leave we're too listless to take the chance. A man knows he's been forgotten back at home, he's a stranger there, a shell in the sea, anyone can tread on him. So he stays, he degenerates and goes to the bad in these hot, humid jungles. It was a bad day when I sold my services to that filthy place …

Not that I did it entirely of my own free will. I had studied in Germany, I was a qualified doctor, indeed a good doctor with a post at the big hospital in Leipzig; in some long-forgotten issue of a medical journal a great deal was made of a new injection that I was the first to introduce. And then I had trouble over a woman, I met her in the hospital; she had driven her lover so crazy that he shot her with a revolver, and soon I was as crazy as he had been. She had a cold, proud manner that drove me to distraction—bold domineering women had always had a hold over me, but she tightened that hold until my bones were breaking. I did what she wanted, I—well, why not say it? It's eight years ago now—I dipped into the hospital funds for her, and when it came out all hell was let loose. An uncle of mine covered up for me when I was dismissed, but my career was over. It was then that I heard the Dutch government was recruiting doctors for the colonies, offering a lump sum in payment. Well, I understood at once the kind of job it would be if they were offering payment like that. For I knew that the crosses on graves in the fever-zone plantations grow three times as fast as at home, but when you're young you think fever and death affect only others. However, I had little choice; I went to Rotterdam, signed up for ten years, and was given a big bundle of banknotes. I sent half home to my uncle, and as for the other half, a woman in the harbour district got it out of me, just because she was so like the vicious cat I'd loved. I sailed away from Europe without money, without even a watch, without illusions, and I wasn't particularly sorry to leave harbour. And then I sat on deck like you, like everyone, and saw the Southern Cross and the palm trees, and my heart rose. Ah, forests, isolation, silence, I dreamed! Well—I'd soon had enough of isolation. I wasn't stationed in Batavia or Surabaya, in a city with other people and clubs, golf, books and newspapers, instead I went to—well, the name doesn't matter—to one of the district stations, two days' journey from the nearest town. A couple of tedious, desiccated officials and a few half-castes were all the society I had, apart from that, nothing for miles around but jungle, plantations, thickets and swamps.

It was tolerable at first. I pursued all kinds of studies; once, when the vice-resident was on a journey of inspection, had a motor accident and broke a leg, I operated on him without assistants, and there was a lot of talk about it. I collected native poisons and weapons, I turned my attention to a hundred little things to keep my mind alert. But that lasted only as long as the strength of Europe was still active in me, and then I dried up. The few Europeans on the station bored me, I stopped mixing with them, I drank and I dreamed. I had only two more years to go before I'd be free, with a pension, and could go back to Europe and begin life again. I wasn't really doing anything but waiting; I lay low and waited. And that's what I would be doing today if she … if it hadn't happened."

The voice in the darkness stopped. The pipe had stopped glowing too. It was so quiet that all of a sudden I could hear the water foaming as it broke against the keel, and the dull, distant throbbing of the engines. I would have liked to light a cigarette, but I was afraid of the bright flash of the lit match and its reflection in his face. He remained silent for a long time. I didn't know if he had finished what he had to say, or was dozing, or had fallen asleep, so profound was his silence.

Then the ship's bell struck a single powerful note: one o'clock. He started. I heard his glass clink again. His hand was obviously feeling around for the whisky. A shot gurgled quietly into his glass, and then the voice suddenly began again, but now it seemed tenser and more passionate.

"So ... wait a moment ... so yes, there I was, sitting in my damned cobweb, I'd been crouching motionless as a spider in its web for months. It was just after the rainy season. Rain had poured down on the roof for weeks on end, not a human being had come along, no European, I'd been stuck there in the house day after day with my yellow-skinned women and my good whisky. I was feeling very 'down' at the time, homesick for Europe. If I read a novel describing clean streets and white women my fingers began to tremble. I can't really describe the condition to you, but it's like a tropical disease, a raging, feverish, yet helpless nostalgia that sometimes comes over a man. So there I was, sitting over an atlas, I think, dreaming of journeys. Then there's a hammering at the door. My boy is there and one of the women, eyes wide with amazement. They make dramatic gestures: there's a woman here, they say, a lady, a white woman.

I jump up in surprise. I didn't hear a carriage or a car approaching. A white woman, here in this wilderness?

I am about to go down the steps, but then I pull myself together. A glance in the mirror, and I hastily tidy myself up a little. I am nervous, restless, I have ominous forebodings, for I know no one in the world who would be coming to visit me out of friendship. At last I go down.

The lady is waiting in the hall, and hastily comes to meet me. A thick motoring veil hides her face. I am about to greet her, but she is quick to get her word in first. 'Good day, doctor,' she says in fluent English—slightly too fluent, as if she had learnt her speech by heart in advance. 'Do forgive me for descending on you like this, but we have just been visiting the station, our car is over there'—here a thought flashes through my mind: why didn't she drive up to the house?—'And then I remembered that you live here. I've heard so much about you—you worked miracles for the vice-resident, his leg is perfectly all right now, he can play golf as well as ever. Oh yes, imagine all of us in the city are still talking about it, we'd happily dispense with our own cross-grained surgeon and the other doctors if you would only come to us instead. Now, why do you never go to the city? You live like a yogi here … '

And so she chatters on, faster and faster, without letting me get a word in. Her loquacity is nervous and agitated, and makes me uneasy. Why is she talking so much, I ask myself, why doesn't she introduce herself, why doesn't she put that veil back? Is she feverish? Is she ill? Is she mad? I feel increasingly nervous, aware that I look ridiculous, standing silently in front of her while her flood of chatter sweeps over me. At last she slows down slightly, and I am able to ask her upstairs. She signs to the boy to stay where he is, and goes up the stairs ahead of me.

'You have a nice place here,' she says, looking around my room. 'Ah, such lovely books! I'd like to read them all!' She goes up to the bookcase and looks at the titles. For the first time since I set eyes on her, she falls silent for a minute.

'May I offer you a cup of tea?' I ask.

She doesn't turn, but just looks at the spines of the books. 'No thank you, doctor ... we have to be off again in a moment, and I don't have much time ... this was just a little detour. Ah, I see you have Flaubert as well, I love him so much ... *L'Education sentimentale*, wonderful, really wonderful ... So you read French too! A man of many talents! Ah, you Germans, you learn everything at school. How splendid to know so many languages! The vice-resident swears by you, he always says he wouldn't go under the knife with anyone else ... our residency surgeon is good for playing bridge but ... the fact is,' she said, still with her face turned away, 'it crossed my mind today that I might consult you myself some time ... and since we happened to be passing anyway, I thought ... oh, but I'm sure you are very busy ... I can come back another time.'

Showing your hand at last, I thought. But I didn't show any reaction, I merely assured her that it would be an honour to be of service to her now or whenever she liked.

'It's nothing serious,' she said, half-turning and at the same time leafing through a book she had taken off the shelf. 'Nothing serious … just small things, women's troubles … dizziness, fainting. This morning I suddenly fainted as we were driving round a bend, fainted right away, the boy had to prop me up in the car and fetch water … but perhaps the chauffeur was just driving too fast, do you think, doctor?'

'I can't say, just like that. Do you often have fainting fits?'

'No … that is, yes … recently, in fact very recently. Yes, I have had such fainting fits, and attacks of nausea.' She is standing in front of the bookcase again, puts the book back, takes another out and riffles the pages. Strange, I think, why does she keep leafing through the pages so nervously, why doesn't she look up behind that veil? Deliberately, I say nothing. I enjoy making her wait. At last she starts talking again in her nonchalant, loquacious way.

'There's nothing to worry about, doctor, is there? No tropical disease … nothing dangerous … ?'

'I'd have to see if you are feverish first. May I take your pulse?'

I approach her, but she moves slightly aside.

'No, no, I'm not feverish … certainly not, certainly not, I've been taking my own temperature every day since … since this fainting began. Never any higher, always exactly 36.4°. And my digestion is healthy too.'

I hesitate briefly. All this time a suspicion has been lurking at the back of my mind: I sense that this woman wants something from me. You certainly don't go into the wilderness to talk about Flaubert. I keep her waiting for a minute or two, then I say, straight out, 'Forgive me, but may I ask you a few frank questions?'

'Of course, doctor! You are a medical man, after all,' she replies, but she has her back turned to me again and is playing with the books.

'Do you have children?'

'Yes, a son.'

'And have you … did you previously … I mean with your son, did you experience anything similar?'

'Yes.'

Her voice is quite different now. Very clear, very firm, no longer loquacious or nervous.

'And is it possible … forgive my asking … that you are now in the same situation?'

'Yes.'

She utters the word in a tone as sharp and cutting as a knife. Her averted head does not move at all.

'Perhaps it would be best, ma'am, if I gave you a general examination. May I perhaps ask you to … to go to the trouble of coming into the next room?'

Then she does turn, suddenly. I feel a cold, determined gaze bent straight on me through her veil.

'No, that won't be necessary … I am fully aware of my condition.'"

The voice hesitated for a moment. The glass that he had refilled shone briefly in the darkness again.

"So listen … but first try to think a little about it for a moment. A woman forces herself on someone who is desperate with loneliness, the first white woman in years to set foot in his room … and suddenly I feel that there

31

is something wrong here, a danger. A shiver runs down my spine: I am afraid of the steely determination of this woman, who arrived with her careless chatter and then suddenly came out with her demand like a knife. For I knew what she wanted me to do, I knew at once—it was not the first time women had made me such requests, but they approached me differently, ashamed or pleading, they came to me with tears and entreaties. But here was a steely … yes, a virile determination. I felt from the first second that this woman was stronger than me, that she could force me to do as she wanted. And yet, and yet … there was some evil purpose in me, a man on his guard, some kind of bitterness, for as I said before … from the first second, indeed even before I had seen her, I sensed that this woman was an enemy.

At first I said nothing. I remained doggedly, grimly silent. I felt that she was looking at me under her veil—looking at me straight and challengingly, I felt that she wanted to force me to speak, but evasively, or indeed unconsciously, I emulated her casual, chattering manner. I acted as if I didn't understand her, for—I don't know if you can understand this—I wanted to force her to speak clearly, I didn't want to offer anything, I wanted to be asked, particularly by her, because her manner was so imperious … and because I knew that I am particularly vulnerable to women with that cold, proud manner.

So I remained non-committal, saying there was no cause for concern, such fainting fits occurred in the natural course of events, indeed they almost guaranteed a happy outcome. I quoted cases from the medical press … I talked and talked, smoothly and effortlessly, always suggesting that this was something very banal, and ... well, I kept waiting for her to interrupt me. Because I knew she wouldn't stand for that.

Then she did interrupt me sharply, waving aside all my reassuring talk.

'That's not what worries me, doctor. When my son was born I was in a better state of health, but now I'm not all right any more ... I have a heart condition ... '

'Ah, a heart condition,' I repeated, apparently concerned. 'We must look into that at once.' And I made as if to stand up and fetch my stethoscope.

But she stopped me again. Her voice was very sharp and firm now—like an officer's on a parade ground.

'I *do* have a heart condition, doctor, and I must ask you to believe what I tell you. I don't want to waste a lot of time with examinations—I think you might show a little more confidence in me. For my part, I've shown sufficient confidence in you.'

Now it was battle, an open challenge, and I accepted it.

'Confidence calls for frank disclosure, with nothing held back. Please speak frankly. I am a doctor. And for heaven's sake take that veil off, sit down, never mind the books and the roundaboutation. You don't go to visit a doctor in a veil.'

Proud and erect, she looked at me. For one moment she hesitated. Then she sat down and lifted her veil. I saw the kind of face I had feared to see, an impenetrable face, hard, controlled, a face of ageless beauty, a face with grey English eyes in which all seemed at peace, and yet behind which one could dream that all was passion. That narrow, compressed mouth gave nothing away if it didn't want to. For a moment we looked at each other—she commandingly and at the same time inquiringly, with such cold, steely cruelty that I couldn't hold her gaze, but instinctively looked away.

She tapped the table lightly with her knuckles. So she was nervous too. Then she said, quickly and suddenly, 'Do you know what I want you to do for me, doctor, or don't you?'

'I believe I do. But let's be quite plain about it. You want an end put to your condition … you want me to cure you of your fainting fits and nausea by … by removing their cause. Is that it?'

'Yes.'

The word fell like a guillotine.

'And do you know that such attempts are dangerous … for both parties concerned?'

'Yes.'

'That I am legally forbidden to do such a thing?'

'There are cases when it isn't forbidden but actually recommended.'

'They call for medical indications, however.'

'Then you'll find such indications. You're a doctor.'

Clear, fixed, unflinching, her eyes looked at me as she spoke. It was an order, and weakling that I am, I trembled with admiration for her demonically imperious will. But I was still evasive, I didn't want to show that I was already crushed. Some spark of desire in me said: don't go too fast! Make difficulties. Force her to beg!

'That is not always within a doctor's competence. But I am ready to ask a colleague at the hospital … '

'I don't want your colleague … I came to you.'

'May I ask why?'

She looked coldly at me. 'I have no reservations about telling you. Because you live in seclusion, because you don't know me—because you are a good doctor, and because,' she added, hesitating for the first time, 'you probably won't stay here very much longer, particularly if you … if you can go home with a large sum of money.'

I felt cold. The adamant, commercial clarity of her calculation bemused me. So far her lips had uttered no request—she had already worked it all out, she had been lying in wait for me and then tracked me down. I felt the demonic force of her will enter into me, but embittered as I was—I resisted. Once again I made myself sound objective, indeed almost ironic.

'Oh, and you would … would place this large sum of money at my disposal?'

'For your help, and then your immediate departure.'

'Do you realise that would lose me my pension?'

'I will compensate you.'

'You're very clear in your mind about it … but I would like even more clarity. What sum did you envisage as a fee?'

'Twelve thousand guilders, payable by cheque when you reach Amsterdam.'

I trembled … I trembled with anger and … yes, with admiration again too. She had worked it all out, the sum and the manner of its payment, which would oblige me to leave this part of the world, she had assessed me and bought me before she even met me, had made arrangements for me in anticipation of getting her own way.

35

I would have liked to strike her in the face, but as I stood there shaking—she too had risen to her feet—and I looked her straight in the eye, the sight of her closed mouth that refused to plead, her haughty brow that would not bend, a ... a kind of violent desire overcame me. She must have felt something of it, for she raised her eyebrows as one would to dismiss a trouble-maker; the hostility between us was suddenly in the open. I knew she hated me because she needed me, and I hated her because ... well, because she would not plead. In that one single second of silence we spoke to each other honestly for the first time. Then an idea suddenly came to me, like the bite of a reptile, and I told her ... I told her ...

But wait a moment, or you'll misunderstand what I did ... what I said. First I must explain how ... well, how that deranged idea came into my mind."

Once again the glass clinked softly in the dark, and the voice became more agitated.

"Not that I want to make excuses, justify myself, clear myself of blame ... but otherwise you won't understand. I don't know if I have ever been what might be called a good man, but ... well, I think I was always helpful. In the wretched life I lived over there, the only pleasure I had was using what knowledge was contained in my brain to keep some living creature breathing ... an almost divine pleasure. It's a fact, those were my happiest moments, for instance when one of the natives came along, pale with

36

fright, his swollen foot bitten by a snake, howling not to have his leg cut off, and I managed to save him. I've travelled for hours to see a woman in a fever—and as for the kind of help my visitor wanted, I'd already given that in the hospital in Europe. But then I could at least feel that these people *needed* me, that I was saving someone from death or despair—and the feeling of being needed was my way of helping myself.

But this woman—I don't know if I can describe it to you—she had irritated and intrigued me from the moment when she had arrived, apparently just strolling casually in. Her provocative arrogance made me resist, she caused everything in me that was—how shall I put it?—everything in me that was suppressed, hidden, wicked, to oppose her. Playing the part of a great lady, meddling in matters of life and death with unapproachable aplomb … it drove me mad. And then … well, after all, no woman gets pregnant just from playing golf. I knew, that is to say I reminded myself with terrible clarity—and this is when my idea came to me—that this cool, haughty, cold woman, raising her eyebrows above her steely eyes if I so much as looked at her askance and parried her demands, had been rolling in bed with a man in the heat of passion two or three months ago, naked as an animal and perhaps groaning with desire, their bodies pressing as close as a pair of lips. That was the idea burning in my mind as she looked at me with such unapproachable coolness, proud as an English army officer … and then everything in me braced itself, I was possessed by the idea of humiliating her. From that moment on, I felt I could see her naked body through her dress …

from that moment on I lived for nothing but the idea of taking her, forcing a groan from her hard lips, feeling this cold, arrogant woman a prey to desire like anyone else, as that other man had done, the man I didn't know. That … that's what I wanted to explain to you. Low as I had sunk, I had never before thought of exploiting such a situation as a doctor … and this time it wasn't desire, the rutting instinct, nothing sexual, I swear it wasn't, I can vouch for it … just a wish to break her pride, dominate her as a man. I think I told you that I have always been susceptible to proud and apparently cold women … and add to that the fact that I had lived here for seven years without sleeping with a white woman, and had met with no resistance … for the girls here, twittering, fragile little creatures who tremble with awe if a white man, a 'master' takes them … they efface themselves in humility, they're always available, always at your service with their soft, gurgling laughter, but that submissive, slavish attitude in itself spoils the pleasure. So can you understand the shattering effect on me when a woman full of pride and hostility suddenly came along, reserved in every fibre of her being, glittering with mystery and at the same time carrying the burden of an earlier passion? When such a woman boldly enters the cage of a man like me, a lonely, starved, isolated brute of a man … well, that's what I wanted to tell you, just so that you'll understand the rest, what happened next. So, full of some kind of wicked greed, poisoned by the thought of her stripped naked, sensuous, submitting, I pulled myself together with pretended indifference. I said coolly, 'Twelve thousand guilders? No, I won't do it for that.'

38

She looked at me, turning a little pale. She probably sensed already that my refusal was not a matter of avarice, but she said, 'Then what do you want?'

I was not putting up with her cool tone any more. 'Let's show our hands, shall we? I am not a tradesman … I'm not the poor apothecary in *Romeo and Juliet* who sells his poison for 'corrupted gold'. Perhaps I'm the opposite of a tradesman … you won't get what you want by those means.'

'So you won't do it?'

'Not for money.'

All was very still between us for a second. So still that for the first time I heard her breathing.

'What else can you want, then?'

Now I could control myself no longer. 'First, I want you to stop … stop speaking to me as if I were a tradesman and address me like a human being. And when you need help, I don't want you to … to come straight out with your shameful offer of money, but to ask me … ask me to help you as one human being to another. I am not just a doctor, I don't spend all my time in consultations … I spend some of it in other ways too, and perhaps you have come at such a time.'

She says nothing for a moment, and then her lip curls very slightly, trembles, and she says quickly, 'Then if I were to ask you … would you do it?'

'You're trying to drive a bargain again—you won't ask me unless I promise first. You must ask me first—then I will give you an answer.'

She tosses her head like a defiant horse, and looks angrily at me.

'No, I will not ask you. I'd rather go to my ruin!'

At that anger seized upon me, red, senseless anger.

'Then if you won't ask, I will make my own demand. I don't think I have to put it crudely—you know what I want from you. And then—then I will help you.'

She stared at me for a moment. Then—oh, I can't, I can't tell you how terrible it was—then her features froze and she ... she suddenly *laughed*, she laughed at me with unspeakable contempt in her face, contempt that was scattered all over me ... and at the same time intoxicated me. That derisive laughter was like a sudden explosion, breaking out so abruptly and with such monstrous force behind it that I ... yes, I could have sunk to the ground and kissed her feet. It lasted only a second ... it was like lightning, and it had set my whole body on fire. Then she turned and went quickly to the door. I instinctively moved to follow her ... to apologise, to beg her ... well, my strength was entirely broken. She turned once more and said ... no, *ordered*, 'Don't dare to follow me or try to track me down. You would regret it.'

And the door slammed shut behind her."

Another hesitation. Another silence ... again, there was only the faint rushing sound, as if of moonlight pouring down. Then, at last, the voice spoke again.

"The door slammed, but I stood there motionless on the spot, as if hypnotized by her order. I heard her go downstairs, open the front door ... I heard it all, and my whole will urged me to follow her ... to ... oh, I don't know what, to call her back, strike her, strangle her, but to follow her … to follow. Yet I couldn't. My limbs were crippled as if by an electric shock … I had been cut to the quick by the imperious gleam of those eyes. I know there's no explaining it, it can't be described … it may sound ridiculous, but I just stood there, and it was several minutes, perhaps five, perhaps ten, before I could raise a foot from the floor …

But no sooner had I moved that foot than I instantly, swiftly, feverishly hurried down the stairs. She could only have gone along the road back to civilisation … I hurry to the shed for my bicycle, I find I have forgotten the door key, I wrench the lock off, splitting and breaking the bamboo of the shed door… and next moment I am on my bicycle and hurrying after her … I have to reach her, I must, before she gets back to her car. I must speak to her. The road rushes past me … only now do I realise how long I must have stood there motionless. Then, where the road through the forest bends just before reaching the buildings of the district station, I see her hurrying along, stepping firmly, walking straight ahead accompanied by her boy … but she must have seen me too, for now she speaks to the boy, who stays behind while she goes on alone. What is she doing? Why does she want to be on her own? Does she want to speak to me out of his hearing? I pedal fast and furiously … then something suddenly springs into my path. It's the boy … I am only just in time to swerve and fall. I rise, cursing … involuntarily I raise my fist to hit the fool, but he leaps aside. I pick up my bicycle to remount it, but then the scoundrel lunges forward, takes hold of the bicycle, and says in his pitiful English, 'You not go on.'

You haven't lived in the tropics … you don't know how unheard-of it is for a yellow bastard like that to seize the bicycle of a white 'master' and tell him, the master, to stay where he is. Instead of answering I strike him in the face with my fist. He staggers, but keeps hold of the bicycle … his eyes, his narrow, frightened eyes are wide open in slavish fear, but he holds the handlebars infernally tight. 'You not go on,' he stammers again. It's lucky I don't have my revolver with me, or I'd shoot him down. 'Out of the way, scum!' is all I say. He cringes and stares at me, but he does not let go of the handlebars. At this rage comes over me … I see that she is well away, she may have escaped me entirely … and I hit him under the chin with a boxer's punch and send him flying. Now I have my bicycle back, but as I jump on it the mechanism jams. A spoke has bent in our tussle. I try to straighten it with trembling hands. I can't, so I fling the bicycle across the road at the scoundrel, who gets up, bleeding, and flinches aside. And then—no, you won't understand how ridiculous it looks to everyone there for a European … well, anyway, I didn't know what I was doing any more. I had only one thought in my mind: to go after her, to reach her. And so I *ran*, ran like a madman along the road and past the huts, where the yellow riff-raff were gathered in amazement to see a white man, the doctor, *running*.

I reach the station, dripping with sweat. My first question is: where is the car? Just driven away … People stare at me in surprise. I must look to them like a lunatic, arriving wet and muddy, screaming my question ahead of me before coming to a halt … Down in the road, I see the white fumes of the car exhaust. She has succeeded …

succeeded, just as all her harsh, cruelly harsh calculations must succeed.

But flight won't help her. There are no secrets among Europeans in the tropics. Everyone knows everyone else, everything is a notable event. And not for nothing did her driver spend an hour in the government bungalow ... in a few minutes, I know all about it. I know who she is, I know that she lives in .... well, in the capital of the colony, eight hours from here by rail. I know that she is ... let's say the wife of a big businessman, enormously rich, distinguished, an Englishwoman. I know that her husband has been in America for five months, and is to arrive here next day to take her back to Europe with him ...

And meanwhile—the thought burns in my veins like poison—meanwhile she can't be more than two or three months pregnant ...

So far I hope I have made it easy for you to understand ... but perhaps only because up to that point I still understood myself, and as a doctor I could diagnose my own condition. From now on, however, something began to work in me like a fever ... I lost control. That's to say, I knew exactly how pointless everything I did was, but I had no power over myself any more ... I no longer understood myself. I was merely racing forward, obsessed by my purpose .... No, wait. Perhaps I can make you understand it after all. Do you know what the expression 'running amok' means?"

" 'Running amok?' Yes, I think I do ... a kind of intoxication affecting the Malays ... "

"It's more than intoxication … it's madness, a sort of human rabies, an attack of murderous, pointless monomania that bears no comparison with ordinary alcohol poisoning. I've studied several cases myself during my time in the East —it's easy to be very wise and objective about other people—but I was never able to uncover the terrible secret of its origin. It may have something to do with the climate, the sultry, oppressive atmosphere that weighs on the nervous system like a storm until it suddenly breaks … well then, this is how it goes: a Malay, an ordinary, good-natured man, sits drinking his brew, impassive, indifferent, apathetic … just as I was sitting in my room … when suddenly he leaps to his feet, snatches his dagger and runs out into the street, going straight ahead of him, always straight ahead, with no idea of any destination. With his *kris* he strikes down anything that crosses his path, man or beast, and this murderous frenzy makes him even more deranged. He froths at the mouth as he runs, he howls like a lunatic … but he still runs and runs and runs, he doesn't look right, he doesn't look left, he just runs on screaming shrilly, brandishing his blood-stained *kris* as he forges straight ahead in that dreadful way. The people of the villages know that no power can halt a man running amok, so they shout warnings ahead when they see him coming —'Amok! Amok!'—and everyone flees … but he runs on without hearing, without seeing, striking down anything he meets … until he is either shot dead like a mad dog or collapses of his own accord, still frothing at the mouth …

I once saw a case from the window of my bungalow. It was a terrible sight, but it's only because I saw it that

I can understand myself in those days ... because I stormed off like that, just like that, obsessed in the same way, going straight ahead with that dreadful expression, seeing nothing to right or to left, following the woman. I don't remember exactly what I did, it all went at such breakneck speed, with such mindless haste ... Ten minutes, no, five—no, two—after I had found out all about the woman, her name, where she lived and her story, I was racing back to my house on a borrowed bicycle, I threw a suit into my case, took some money and drove to the railway station in my carriage. I went without informing the district officer, without finding a locum for myself, I left the house just as it was, unlocked. The servants were standing around, the astonished women were asking questions. I didn't answer, didn't turn, drove to the station and took the next train to the city ... only an hour after that woman had entered my room, I had thrown my life away and was running amok, careering into empty space.

I ran straight on, headlong ... I arrived in the city at six in the evening, and at ten past six I was at her house asking to see her. It was ... well, as you will understand, it was the most pointless, stupid thing I could have done, but a man runs amok with empty eyes, he doesn't see where he is going. The servant came back after a few minutes, cool and polite: his mistress was not well and couldn't see anyone.

I staggered away. I prowled around the house for an hour, possessed by the insane hope that she might perhaps come looking for me. Only then did I book into the hotel on the beach and went to my room with two bottles of whisky which, with a double dose of veronal, helped to calm me. At last I fell asleep … and that dull, troubled sleep was the only momentary respite in my race between life and death."

The ship's bell sounded. Two hard, full strokes that vibrated on, trembling, in the soft pool of near-motionless air and then ebbed away in the quiet, endless rushing of the water washing around the keel, its sound mingling with his passionate tale. The man opposite me in the dark must have started in alarm, for his voice hesitated. Once again I heard his hand move down to find a bottle, and the soft gurgling. Then, as if reassured, he began again in a firmer voice.

"I can scarcely tell you about the hours I passed from that moment on. I think, today, that I was in a fever at the time; at the least I was in a state of over-stimulation bordering on madness—as I told you, I was running amok. But don't forget, it was Tuesday night when I arrived, and on Saturday—as I had now discovered—her husband was to arrive on the P&O steamer from Yokohama. So there were just three days left, three brief days for the decision to be made and for me to help her. You'll understand that I knew I must help her at once, yet I couldn't speak a word to her. And my need to apologise for my ridiculous, deranged behaviour drove me on. I knew how valuable every moment was, I knew it was a matter of life and death to her, yet I had no opportunity of approaching her with so much as a whisper or a sign, because my tempestuous foolishness in chasing after her had frightened her off. It was … wait, yes … it was like running after someone warning that a murderer is on the way, and that person thinks you are the murderer yourself and so runs on to ruin … She saw me only as a man running amok, pursuing her in order to humiliate her, but I … and this was the terrible absurdity of it … I wasn't thinking of that any more at all. I was destroyed already, I just wanted to help her, do her a service. I would have committed murder, any crime, to help her … but she didn't understand that. When I woke in the morning and went straight back to her house, the boy was standing in the doorway, the servant whose face I had punched, and when he saw me coming—he must have been looking out for me—he hurried in through the door. Perhaps he went in only to announce my arrival discreetly … perhaps … oh, that uncertainty, how it torments me now … perhaps everything was ready to receive me, but then, when I saw him, I remembered my disgrace, and this time I didn't even dare to try calling on her again. I was weak at the knees. Just before reaching the doorway I turned and went away again … went away, while she, perhaps, was waiting for me in a similar state of torment.

I didn't know what to do in this strange city that seemed to burn like fire beneath my feet. Suddenly I thought of something, called for a carriage, went to see the vice-resident on whose leg I had operated back at my own district station, and had myself announced. Something in my appearance must have seemed strange, for he looked at me with slight alarm, and there was an uneasiness about his civility … perhaps he recognised me as a man running amok. I told him, briefly, that I wanted a transfer to the city, I couldn't exist in my present post any longer, I said, I had to move at once. He looked at me … I can't tell you how he looked at me … perhaps as a doctor looks at a sick man. 'A nervous breakdown, my dear doctor?' he said. 'I understand that only too well. I'm sure it can be arranged, but wait … let's say for four weeks, while I find a replacement.'

'I can't wait, I can't wait even a day,' I replied. Again he gave me that strange look. 'You must, doctor,' he said gravely. 'We can't leave the station without a medical man. But I promise you I'll set everything in motion this very day.' I stood there with my teeth gritted; for the first time I felt clearly that I was a man whose services had been bought, I was a slave. I was preparing to defy him when, diplomat that he was, he got his word in first. 'You're unused to mixing with other people, doctor, and in the end that becomes an illness. We've all been surprised that you never came here to the city or went on leave. You need more company, more stimulation. Do at least come to the government reception this evening. You'll find the entire colony, and many of them have long wanted to meet you, they've often asked about you and hoped to see you here.'

That last remark pulled me up short. People had asked about me? Could he mean *her*? I was suddenly a different man: I immediately thanked him courteously for his invitation and assured him that I would be there punctually. And punctual I was, over-punctual. I hardly have to tell you that, driven by my impatience, I was the first in the great hall of the government building, surrounded by the silent, yellow-skinned servants whose bare feet hurried back and forth, and who—so it seemed to me in my confused state of mind—were laughing at me behind my back. For a quarter of an hour I was the only European among all the soundless preparations, so alone with myself that I could hear the ticking of my watch in my waistcoat pocket. Then a few government officials at last appeared with their families, and finally the Governor too entered, and drew me into a long conversation in which I assiduously and I think skilfully played my part, until … until suddenly, attacked by a mysterious attack of nerves, I lost all my diplomatic manner and began stammering. Although my back was to the entrance of the hall, I suddenly felt that she must have entered and was present there. I can't tell you how that sudden certainty confused me, but even as I was talking to the Governor and heard his words echo in my ears, I sensed her presence somewhere behind me. Luckily the Governor soon ended the conversation—or I think I would suddenly and abruptly have turned, so strong was that mysterious tugging of my nerves, so burning and agitated my desire. And sure enough, I had hardly turned before I saw her exactly where my senses had unconsciously guessed she would be. She wore a yellow ball-dress that made her slender, immaculate shoulders glow like dull ivory, and was talking to a group of guests. She was smiling, but I thought there was a tense expression on her face. I came closer—she either could not or would not see me—and looked at the attractive smile civilly hovering on her narrow lips. And that smile intoxicated me again, because … well, because I knew it was a lie born of art or artifice, a masterpiece of deception. Today is Wednesday, I thought, on Saturday the ship with her husband on board will arrive ... how can she smile like that, so ... so confidently, with such a carefree look, casually playing with the fan she holds instead of crushing it in her fear? I ... I, a stranger, had been trembling for two days at the thought of this moment ... Strange to her as I was, I experienced her fear and horror intensely ... and she herself went to this ball and smiled, smiled, smiled ...

Music started to play at the back of the hall. The dancing began. An elderly officer had asked her to dance; she left the chattering circle with a word of excuse and walked on his arm towards the other hall and past me. When she saw me her face suddenly froze—but only for a second, and then, before I could make up my mind whether or not to greet her, she gave me a civil nod of recognition, as she would to a chance acquaintance, said, 'Good evening, doctor,' and was gone. No one could have guessed what that grey-green glance concealed; I didn't know myself. Why did she speak to me ... why did she suddenly acknowledge me? Was it rejection, was it a *rapprochement*, was it just the embarrassment of surprise? I can't describe the agitation into which I was cast; everything was in turmoil, explosively concentrated within me, and as I saw her like that—casually waltzing in the officer's arms, with such a cool, carefree look on her brow, while I knew that she ... that she, like me, was thinking of only one thing ... that we two alone, out of everyone here, had a terrible secret in common ... and she was waltzing ... well, in those few seconds my fear, my longing and my admiration became more passionate than ever. I don't know if anyone was watching me, but certainly my conduct gave away no more than hers—I just could not look in any other direction, I had to … I absolutely had to look at her from a distance, my eyes fastening on her closed face to see if the mask would not drop for a second. She must have found the force of my gaze uncomfortable. As she moved away on her dancing partner's arm, she glanced my way for a split second with imperious sharpness, as if repelling me; once again that little frown of haughty anger, the one I knew already, disfigured her brow.

But … but, as I told you, I was running amok; I looked neither to right nor to left. I understood her at once—her glance said: don't attract attention! Control yourself! I knew that she … how can I put it? … that she expected me to behave discreetly here in the hall, in public. I realised that if I went home at this point, I could be certain she would see me in the morning … that all she wanted to avoid just now was being exposed to my obvious familiarity with her, I knew she feared—and rightly—that my clumsiness would cause a scene. You see, I knew everything, I understood that imperious grey gaze, but … but my feelings were too strong, I had to speak to her. So I moved unsteadily over to the group where she stood talking, joined its loose-knit circle although I knew only a few of the people in it, merely in the hope of hearing her speak, yet always flinching from her eyes timidly, like a whipped dog, when they coldly rested on me as if I were one of the linen curtains hanging behind me, or the air that lightly moved it. But I stood there thirsty for a word spoken to me, for a sign of our understanding, I stood like a block, gazing at her amidst all the chatter. It cannot have passed unnoticed, for no one addressed a word to me, and she had to suffer my ridiculous presence.

I don't know how long I would have stood there ... for ever, perhaps ... I *could* not leave that enchantment of my own volition. The very force of my frenzy crippled me. But she could not bear it any more ... she suddenly turned to the gentlemen, with the magnificent ease that came naturally to her, and said, 'I am a little tired ... I think I'll go to bed early for once. Good night!' And she was walking past me with a distant social nod of her head ... I could still see the frown on her face, and then nothing but her back, her white, cool, bare back. It was a second before I realised that she was leaving ... that I wouldn't be able to see her or speak to her again this evening, this last evening before I could help her. For a moment I stood there rooted to the spot until I realised it, and then ... then ...

But wait ... wait, or you will not understand how stupid and pointless what I did was. I must describe the whole room to you first. It was the great hall of the government building, entirely illuminated by lights and almost empty ... the couples had gone into the other room to dance, gentlemen had gone to play cards ... only a few groups were still talking in the corners, so the hall was empty, every movement conspicuous and visible in the bright light. And she walked slowly and lightly through that great hall with her shoulders straight, exchanging greetings now and then with indescribable composure, with the magnificent, frozen, proud calm that so enchanted me. I ... I had stayed behind, as I told you, as if paralysed, before I realised that she was leaving ... and then, when I did realise, she was already at the far side of the hall and just approaching the doors. Then … and I am still ashamed to think of it now … something suddenly came over me and I *ran* … I ran, do you hear? … I did not walk but *ran* through the hall after her, my shoes clattering on the floor. I heard my own footsteps, I saw all eyes turning to me in surprise … I could have died of shame … even as I ran I understood my own derangement, but I could not … could not go back now. I caught up with her in the doorway. She turned to me … her eyes stabbed like grey steel, her nostrils were quivering with anger … I was just going to stammer something out when … when she suddenly *laughed* aloud … a clear, carefree, whole-hearted laugh, and said, in a voice loud enough for everyone to hear, 'Oh, doctor, have you only just remembered my little boy's prescription? Ah, you learned scientists!' A couple of people standing nearby laughed kindly … I understood, and was shattered by the masterly way she had saved the situation. I put my hand in my wallet and tore a blank leaf off my prescription block, and she took it casually before … again with a cold smile of thanks … before she went. For one second I felt easy in my mind… I saw that her skill in dealing with my blunder had made up for it and put things right—but next moment I also knew that all was over for me now, she hated me for my intemperate folly … hated me worse than death itself. I could come to her door hundreds upon hundreds of times, and she would always have me turned away like a dog.

I staggered through the room … I realised that people were looking at me, and I must have appeared strange. I went to the buffet and drank two, three, four glasses of cognac one after another, which saved me from collapsing.

My nerves could bear no more, they were in shreds. Then I slunk out through a side entrance, as secretly as a criminal. Not for any principality in the world could I have walked back through that hall, with her carefree laughter still echoing from its walls. I went ... I really can't say now exactly where I went, but into a couple of bars where I got drunk, like a man trying to drink his consciousness away ... but I could not numb my senses, the laughter was there in me, high and dreadful ... I could not silence that damned laughter. I wandered around the harbour ... I had left my revolver in my room, or I would have shot myself. I could think of nothing else, and with that thought I went back to the hotel with one idea in my mind ... the left-hand drawer of the chest where my revolver lay ... with that single idea in mind.

The fact that I didn't shoot myself after all ... I swear it wasn't cowardice, it would have been a release to take off the safety catch and press the cold trigger ... how can I explain it? I still felt I had a duty ... yes, that damned duty to help. The thought that she might still need me, that she did need me, made me mad ... it was Thursday morning before I was back in my room, and on Saturday, as I have told you, on Saturday the ship would come in, and I knew that *this* woman, this proud and haughty woman would not survive being shamed before her husband and the world ... Oh, how my thoughts tortured me, thoughts of the precious time I had unthinkingly wasted, the crazy haste that had thwarted any prospect of bringing her help in time ... for hours, I swear, for hours on end I paced up and down my room, racking my brains to think of a way to approach her, put matters right, help her ... for I was certain that she wouldn't let me into her house now. Her laughter was still there in all my nerves, I still saw her nostrils quivering with anger. For hours I paced up and down the three metres of my cramped room ... and day had dawned, morning was here already.

Suddenly an idea sent me to the desk ... I snatched up a sheaf of notepaper and began to write to her, write it all down ... a whining, servile letter in which I begged her forgiveness, called myself a madman, a criminal, and begged her to entrust herself to me. I swore that the hour after it was done I would disappear from the city, from the colony, from the world if she wanted ... only she must forgive me and trust me to help her at the last, the very last minute. I feverishly wrote twenty pages like this ... it must have been a mad, indescribable letter, like a missive written in delirium, for when I rose from the desk I was bathed in sweat ... the room swayed, and I had to drink a glass of water. Only then did I try reading the letter through again, but the very first words horrified me, so I folded it up, trembling, found an envelope ... and suddenly a new thought came to me. All at once I knew the right, the crucial thing to say. I picked up the pen again, and wrote on the last sheet, 'I will wait here in the beach hotel for a word of forgiveness. If no answer comes by seven this evening, I shall shoot myself.'

Then I took the letter, rang for a boy, and told him to deliver the envelope at once. At last I had said everything—everything!"

Something clinked and fell down beside us. As he moved abruptly he had knocked over the whisky bottle; I heard his hand feeling over the deck for it, and then he picked it up with sudden vigour. He threw the empty bottle high in the air and over the ship's side. The voice fell silent for a few minutes, and then feverishly continued, even faster and more agitated than before.

"I am not a believing Christian any more … I don't believe in heaven or hell, and if hell does exist I am not afraid of it, for it can't be worse than those hours I passed between morning and evening … think of a small room, hot in the sunlight, red-hot at blazing noon … a small room, just a desk and a chair and the bed … and nothing on the desk but a watch and a revolver, and sitting at the desk a man … a man who does nothing but stare at that desk and the second hand of his watch, a man who eats and drinks nothing, doesn't smoke, doesn't move, who only … listen to me … who only stares for three long hours at the white circle of the dial and the hand of the watch ticking as it goes around. That … that was how I spent the day, just waiting, waiting, waiting … but waiting like a man running amok, senselessly, like an animal, with that headlong, direct persistence.

Well, I won't try to describe those hours to you … they are beyond description. I myself don't understand now how one can go through such an experience without going mad. Then, at twenty-two minutes past three … I remember the time exactly, I was staring at my watch … there was a sudden knock at the door. I leap up … leap like a tiger leaping on its prey, in one bound I am across the room and at the door, I fling it open, and there stands a timid little Chinese boy with a folded note in his hand. As I avidly reach for it, he scurries away and is gone.

I tear the note open to read it ... and find that I can't. A red mist blurs my vision ... imagine my agony, I have word from her at last, and now everything is quivering and dancing before my eyes. I dip my head in water, and my sight clears ... once again I take the note and read it. "Too late! But wait where you are. I may yet send for you."

No signature on the crumpled paper torn from some old brochure ... the writing of someone whose handwriting is usually steady, now scribbling hastily, untidily, in pencil. I don't know why that note shook me so much. Some kind of horror, some mystery clung to it, it might have been written in flight, by someone standing in a window bay or a moving vehicle. An unspeakably cold aura of fear, haste and terror about that furtive note chilled me to the heart ... and yet, and yet I was happy. She had written to me, I need not die yet, I could help her ... perhaps I could ... oh, I lost myself in the craziest hopes and conjectures. I read the little note a hundred, a thousand times over, I kissed it ... I examined it for some word I might have forgotten or overlooked. My reverie grew ever deeper and more confused, I was in a strange condition, sleeping with open eyes, a kind of paralysis, a torpid yet turbulent state between sleep and waking. It lasted perhaps for quarter of an hour or so, perhaps for hours.

Suddenly I gave a start. Wasn't that a knock at the door? I held my breath for a minute, two minutes of perfect silence ... and then it came again, like a mouse nibbling, a soft but urgent knock. I leaped to my feet, still dizzy, flung the door open, and there outside it stood her boy, the same boy whom I had once struck in the face with my fist. His brown face was pale as ashes, his confused glance spoke of some misfortune. I immediately felt horror. 'What ... what's happened?' I managed to stammer. He said, 'Come quickly!' That was all, no more, but I was immediately racing down the stairs with the boy after me. A *sado*, a kind of small carriage, stood waiting. We got in. 'What's happened?' I asked him. He looked at me, trembling, and remained silent, lips compressed. I asked again ... still he was silent. I could have struck him with my fist once more, but his doglike devotion to her touched me, and I asked no more questions. The little carriage trotted through the crowded street so fast that people scattered, cursing. It left the European quarter near the beach in the lower town and went on into the noisy turmoil of the city's Chinatown district. At last we reached a narrow, very remote alley ... and the carriage stopped outside a low-built house. The place was dirty, with a kind of hunched look about it and a little shop window where a tallow candle stood ... one of those places where you would expect to find opium dens or brothels, a thieves' lair or a receivers' cellar full of stolen goods. The boy quickly knocked ... a voice whispered through a crack in the door, which stood ajar, there were questions and more questions. I could stand it no longer. I leaped up, pushed the door right open, and an old Chinese woman shrank back with a little scream. The boy followed me, led me along the passage ... opened another door ... another door, leading to a dark room with a foul smell of brandy and clotted blood. Something in the room groaned. I groped my way in ... "

Once again his voice failed. And what he next uttered was more of a sob than words.

"I ... I groped my way in .... And there ... there on a dirty mat, doubled up with pain ... a groaning piece of human flesh ... there she lay ...

I couldn't see her face in the darkness. My eyes weren't yet used to it ... so I only groped about and found ... found her hand, hot, burning hot ... she had a temperature, a very high one, and I shuddered, for I instantly knew it all ... how she had fled here from me, had let some dirty Chinese woman mutilate her, only because she hoped for more silence in that quarter ... she had allowed some diabolical witch to murder her rather than trust me ... because, deranged as I was, I hadn't spared her pride, I hadn't helped her at once ... because she feared me more than she feared death.

I shouted for light. The boy ran off; the appalling Chinese woman, her hands trembling, brought a smoking oil lamp. I had to stop myself taking her by her filthy yellow throat as she put the lamp on the table. Its light fell bright and yellow on the tortured body. And suddenly ... suddenly all my emotions were gone, all my apathy, my anger, all the impure filth of my accumulated passion ... I was nothing but a doctor now, a human being who could understand and feel and help. I had forgotten myself, I was fighting the horror of it with my senses alert and clear ... I felt the naked body I had desired in my dreams only as ... how can I put it? ... as matter, an organism. I did not see *her* any more, only life defending itself against death, a human being bent double in dreadful agony. Her blood, her hot, holy blood streamed over my hands, but I felt no desire and no horror, I was only a doctor. I saw only her suffering ... and I saw ...

And I saw at once that barring a miracle, all was lost ... the woman's criminally clumsy hand had injured her, and she had bled half to death ... and I had nothing to stop the bleeding in that stinking den, not even clean water. Everything I touched was stiff with dirt ...

'We must go straight to the hospital,' I said. But no sooner had I spoken than her tortured body reared convulsively.

'No ... no ... would rather die ... no one must know ... no one ... home ... home ... '

I understood. She was fighting now only to keep her secret, to preserve her honour ... not to save her life. And—and I obeyed. The boy brought a litter, we placed her in it ... and so we carried her home, already like a corpse, limp and feverish, through the night, fending off the frightened servants' inquiries. Like thieves, we carried her into her own room and closed the doors. And then ... then the battle began, the long battle with death ... "

Suddenly a hand clutched my arm, and I almost cried out with the shock and pain of it. His face in the dark was suddenly hideously close to mine, I saw his white teeth gleam in his sudden outburst, saw his glasses shine like two huge cat's eyes in the pale reflection of the moonlight. And now he was not talking any more but screaming, shaken by howling rage.

"Do you know, stranger, sitting here so casually in your deckchair, travelling at leisure around the world, do you know what it's like to watch someone dying? Have you even been at a deathbed, have you seen the body contort, blue nails scrabbling at the empty air while breath rattles in the dying throat, every limb fights back, every finger is braced against the terror of it, and the eye stares into horror for which there are no words? Have you ever experienced that, idle tourist that you are, you who call it a duty to help? As a doctor I've often seen it, seen it as ... as a clinical case, a fact ... I have studied it, so to speak—but I *experienced* it only once, there with her, I died with her that night ... that dreadful night when I sat there racking my brains to think of something, some way to staunch the blood that kept on flowing, soothe the fever consuming her before my eyes, ward off death as it came closer and closer, and I couldn't keep it from her bed. Can you guess what it means to be a doctor, to know how to combat every illness—to feel the duty of helping, as you so sagely put it, and yet to sit helpless by a dying woman, knowing what is happening but powerless ... just knowing the one terrible truth, that there is nothing you can do, although you would open every vein in your own body for her? Watching a beloved body bleed miserably to death in agonising pain, feeling a pulse that flutters and grows faint ... ebbing away under your fingers. To be a doctor yet know of nothing, nothing, nothing you can do … just sitting there stammering out some kind of prayer like an little old lady in church, shaking your fist in the face of a merciful god who you know doesn't exist … can you understand that? Can you understand it? There's just one thing I don't understand myself: how … how a man can manage not to die too at such moments, but wake from sleep the next morning, clean his teeth, put on a tie … go on living, when he has experienced what I felt as her breath failed, as the first human being for whom I was really wrestling, fighting, whom I wanted to keep alive with all the force of my being … as she slipped away from me to somewhere else, faster and faster, minute after minute, and my feverish brain could do nothing to keep that one woman alive …

And then, to add to my torment, there was something else too … as I sat at her bedside—I had given her morphine to relieve the pain—and I saw her lying there with burning cheeks, hot and ashen, as I sat there, I felt two eyes constantly fixed on me from behind, gazing at me with terrible expectation. The boy sat there on the floor, quietly murmuring some kind of prayer, and when my eyes met his I saw … oh, I cannot describe it … I saw something so pleading, so … so grateful in his doglike gaze! And at the same time he raised his hands to me as if urging me to save her … to me, you understand, he raised his hands to *me* as if to a god … to me, the helpless weakling who knew the battle was lost, that I was as useless here as an ant scuttling over the floor. How that gaze tormented me, that fanatical, animal hope of what my art could do … I could have shouted at him, kicked him, it hurt so much … and yet I felt that we were both linked by our love for her ... by the secret. A waiting animal, an apathetic tangle of limbs, he sat hunched up just behind me. The moment I asked for anything he leaped to his bare, silent feet and handed it to me, trembling ... expectantly, as if that might help, might save her. I know he would have cut his veins to help her ... she was that kind of woman, she had such power over people ... and I ... I didn't even have the power to save her from bleeding ... oh, that night, that appalling night, an endless night spent between life and death!

Towards morning she woke again and opened her eyes ... they were not cold and proud now ... there was a moist gleam of fever in them as they looked around the room, as if it were strange ... Then she looked at me. She seemed to be thinking, trying to remember my face ... and suddenly, I saw, she did remember, because some kind of shock, rejection ... a hostile, horrified expression came over her features. She flailed her arms as if to flee ... far, far away from me ... I saw she was thinking of *that* ... of the time back at my house. But then she thought again and looked at me more calmly, breathing heavily ... I felt that she wanted to speak, to say something. Again her hands began to flex ... she tried to sit up, but she was too weak. I calmed her, leaned down to her ... and she gave me a long and tormented look ... her lips moved slightly in a last, failing sound as she said, 'Will no one ever know? No one?'

'No one,' I said, with all the strength of my conviction. 'I promise you.'

But her eyes were still restless. Her fevered lips managed, indistinctly, to get it out.

'Swear to me ... that no one will know ... swear.'

I raised my hand as if taking an oath. She looked at me with ... with an indescribable expression... it was soft, warm, grateful ... yes, truly, truly grateful. She tried to say something else, but it was too difficult for her. She lay there for a long time, exhausted by the effort, with her eyes closed. Then the terrible part began ... the terrible part ... she fought for another entire and difficult hour. Not until morning was it all over ... "

He was silent for some time. I did not notice until the bell struck from amidships, once, twice, three times—three o'clock. The moon was not shining so brightly now, but a different, faint yellow glow was already trembling in the air, and the wind blew light as a breeze from time to time. Half-an-hour more, an hour more, and it would be day, the grey around us would be extinguished by clear light. I saw his features more distinctly now that the shadows were not so dense and dark in the corner where we sat—he had taken off his cap, and now that his head was bared his tormented face looked even more terrible. But already the gleaming lenses of his glasses were turned to me again, he pulled himself together, and his voice took on a sharp and derisive tone.

"It was all over for her now—but not for me. I was alone with the body—but I was also alone in a strange house and in a city that would permit no secrets, and I ... I had to keep hers. Think about it, think about the circumstances: a woman from the colony's high society, a perfectly healthy woman who had been dancing at the government ball only the evening before, suddenly dead in her bed ... and a strange doctor with her, apparently called by her servant ... no one in the house saw when he arrived or where he came from ... she was carried in by night in a litter, and then the doors were closed ... and in the morning she was dead. Only then were the servants called, and suddenly the house echoes with screams ... the neighbours will know at once, the whole city will know, and there's only one man who can explain it all ... I, the stranger, the doctor from a remote country station. A delightful situation, don't you agree?

I knew what lay ahead of me now. Fortunately the boy was with me, the good fellow who read every thought of mine in my eyes—that yellow-skinned, dull-minded creature knew that there was still a battle to be fought. I had said to him only, 'Your mistress did not want anyone to know what happened.' He returned my glance with his moist, doglike, yet determined gaze. All he said was, 'Yes, sir.' But he washed the blood off the floor, tidied every-thing—and his very determination restored mine to me.

Never in my life before, I know, was I master of such concentrated energy, and I never shall be again. When you have lost everything, you fight desperately for the last that is left—and the last was her legacy to me, my obli-gation to keep her secret. I calmly received the servants, told them all the same invented story: how the boy she had sent for the doctor happened to meet me by chance on his way. But while I talked, apparently calmly, I was waiting ... waiting all the time for the crucial appearance of the medical officer who would have to make out the death certificate before we could put her in her coffin, and her secret with her. Don't forget, this was Thursday, and her husband would arrive on Saturday …

At last, at nine o'clock, I heard the medical officer announced. I had told the servants to send for him—he was my superior in rank and at the same time my rival, the same doctor of whom she had once spoken with such contempt, and who had obviously already heard about my application for a transfer. I sensed his hostility at once, but that in itself stiffened my backbone.

In the front hall he immediately asked, 'When did Frau … naming her by her surname—when did she die?'

'At six in the morning.'

'When did she send for you?'

'Eleven last night.'

'Did you know that I was her doctor?'

'Yes, but this was an emergency … and then … well, she asked especially for me. She wouldn't let them call any other doctor.'

He stared at me, and a flush of red came into his pale, rather plump face. I could tell that he felt bitter. But that was exactly what I needed—all my energies were concentrating on getting a quick decision, for I could feel that my nerves wouldn't hold out much longer. He was going to return a hostile reply, but then said more mildly, 'You may think that you can dispense with my services, but it is still my official duty to confirm death—and establish the cause of death.'

I did not reply, but let him go into the room ahead of me. Then I stepped back, locked the door and put the key on the table. He raised his eyebrows in surprise.

'What's the meaning of this?'

I faced him calmly. 'We don't have to establish the cause of death, we have to think of a different one. This lady called me to treat her after … after suffering the consequences of an operation that went wrong. It was too late for me to save her, but I promised I would save her reputation, and that is what I'm going to do. And I am asking you to help me.'

His eyes were wide with astonishment. 'You surely aren't saying,' he stammered, 'that you're asking me, as medical officer, to conceal a crime?'

'Yes, I am. I must.'

'So I'm to pay for your crime?'

'I've told you, I didn't touch this lady, or … or I wouldn't be here talking to you, I would have put an end to myself by now. She has paid for her transgression, if that's what you want to call it. There's no need for the world to know about it. And I will not allow this lady's reputation to be tarnished now for no good reason.'

My firm tone made him even angrier. 'You will not allow … oh, so I suppose you're my superior, or at least you think you are! Just try giving me orders … when you were summoned here from your country outpost I thought at once there was something fishy going on … nice practices you get up to, I must say, here's a pretty sample of your skill! But now *I* will examine her, *I* will do it, and you may depend upon it that any account to which my name is signed will be correct. I won't put my name to a lie.'

I kept quite calm. 'This time you must. You won't leave the room until you do.'

I put my hand in my pocket. In fact I did not have my revolver with me, but he jumped in alarm. I came a step closer and looked at him.

'Listen, let me tell you something ... and then we need not resort to desperate measures. I have reached a point where I set no store by my life or anyone else's ... I am anxious only to keep my promise that the manner of this death will remain secret. And listen to this too: I give you my word of honour that if you will sign the certificate saying that this lady died of ... well, died accidentally, I will leave this city and the East Indies too in the course of this week ... and if you want, I will take my revolver and shoot myself as soon as the coffin is in the ground and I can be sure that no one... *no one*, you understand—can make any more inquiries. That ought to satisfy you—it *must* satisfy you.'

There must have been something menacing in my voice, something quite dangerous, because as I instinctively came closer he retreated with the obvious horror of ... of someone fleeing from a man in frenzy running amok, wielding a *kris*. And suddenly he had changed ... he cringed, so to speak, he was bemused, his hard attitude crumbled. He murmured something with a last faint protest. 'It will be the first time in my life that I've signed a false certificate ... still, I expect some form of words can be found ... Who knows what would happen if ... but I can't simply ... '

'Of course not,' I said helpfully, to strengthen his will—only move fast, move fast, said the tingling sensation in my temples—'but now that you know you would only be hurting a living man and doing a terrible injury to a dead woman, I am sure you will not hesitate.'

He nodded. We approached the table. A few minutes

68

later the certificate was made out; it was published later in the newspaper, and told a credible story of a heart attack. Then he rose and looked at me.

'And you'll leave this week, then?'

'My word of honour.'

He looked at me again. I realised that he wanted to appear stern and objective. 'I'll see about a coffin at once,' he said, to hide his embarrassment. But whatever it was about me that made me so ... so dreadful, so tormented—he suddenly offered me his hand and shook mine with hearty good feeling. 'I hope you will be better soon,' he said—I didn't know what he meant. Was I sick? Was I ... was I mad? I accompanied him to the door and unlocked it—and it was with the last of my strength that I closed it again behind him. Then the tingling in my temples returned, everything swayed and went round before my eyes, and I collapsed beside her bed ... just as a man running amok falls senseless at the end of his frenzied career, his nerves broken."

Once again he paused. I shivered slightly: was it the first shower carried on the morning wind that blew softly over the deck? But the tormented face, now partly visible in the reflected light of dawn, was getting control of itself again.

"I don't know how long I lay on the mat like that. Then someone touched me. I came to myself with a start. It was the boy, timidly standing before me with his look of devotion and gazing uneasily at me.

'Someone wants come in ... wants see her ... '

'No one may come in.'

'Yes ... but ... '

There was alarm in his eyes. He wanted to say something, but dared not. The faithful creature was in some kind of torment.

'Who is it?'

He looked at me, trembling as if he feared a blow. And then he said—he named a name—how does such a lowly creature suddenly come by so much knowledge, how is it that at some moments these dull human souls show unspeakable tenderness?—then he said, very, very timidly, 'It is *him*.'

I started again, understood at once, and I was immediately avid, impatient to set eyes on the unknown man. For strangely enough, you see, in the midst of all my agony, my fevered longing, fear and haste, I had entirely forgotten 'him', I had forgotten there was a man involved too ... the man whom this woman had loved, to whom she had passionately given what she denied to me. Twelve, twenty-four hours ago I would still have hated him, I would have been ready to tear him to pieces. Now ... well, I can't tell you how much I wanted to see him, to ... to love him because she had loved him.

I was suddenly at the door. There stood a young, very young fair-haired officer, very awkward, very slender, very pale. He looked like a child, so ... so touchingly young, and I was unutterably shaken to see how hard he was trying to be a man and maintain his composure, hide his emotion. I saw at once that his hands were trembling as he raised them to his cap. I could have embraced him ... because he was so exactly what I would have wished the man who had possessed her to be, not a seducer, not proud ... no, still half a child, a pure, affectionate creature to whom she had given herself.

The young man stood before me awkwardly. My avid glance, my passionate haste as I rushed to let him in confused him yet more. The small moustache on his upper lip trembled treacherously ... this young officer, this child, had to force himself not to sob out loud.

'Forgive me,' he said at last. 'I would have liked to see Frau ... I would so much have liked to see her again.'

Unconsciously, without any deliberate intention, I put my arm around the young stranger's shoulders and led him in as if he were an invalid. He looked at me in surprise, with an infinitely warm and grateful expression ... at that moment, some kind of understanding existed between the two of us of what we had in common. We went over to the dead woman. There she lay, white-faced, in white linen—I felt that my presence troubled him, so I stepped back to leave him alone with her. He went slowly closer with ... with such reluctant, hesitant steps. I saw from the set of his shoulders the kind of turmoil that was ranging in him. He walked like ... like a man walking into a mighty gale. And suddenly he fell to his knees beside the bed, just as I had done.

I came forward at once, raised him and led him to an armchair. He was not ashamed any more, but sobbed out his grief. I could say nothing—I just instinctively stroked his fair, childishly soft hair. He reached for my hand ... very gently, yet anxiously ... and suddenly I felt his eyes on me. 'Tell me the truth, doctor,' he stammered. 'Did she lay hands on herself?'

'No,' I said.

'And … I mean … is anyone … is someone to blame for her death?'

'No,' I said again, although a desire was rising in me to cry out, 'I am! I am! I am! And so are you! The pair of us! And her obstinacy, her ill-starred obstinacy.' But I controlled myself. I repeated, 'No … no one is to blame. It was fate!'

'I can't believe it,' he groaned, 'I can't believe it. She was at the ball only the day before yesterday, she waved to me. How is it possible, how could it happen?'

I told a lengthy lie. I did not betray her secret even to him. We talked together like two brothers over the next few days, as if irradiated by the emotion that bound us … we did not confess it to each other, but we both felt that our whole lives had depended on that woman. Sometimes the truth rose to my lips, choking me, but I gritted my teeth, and he never learned that she had been carrying his child, or that I had been asked to kill the child, his offspring, and she had taken it down into the abyss with her. Yet we talked of nothing but her in those days, when I was hiding away with him—for I forgot to tell you that they were looking for me. Her husband had arrived after the coffin was closed, and wouldn't accept the medical findings. There were all kinds of rumours, and he was looking for me … but I couldn't bear to see him when I knew that she had suffered in her marriage to him … I hid away, for four days I didn't go out of the house, we neither of us left her lover's apartment. He had booked me a passage under a false name so that I could get away easily. I went on board by night, like a thief, in case anyone recognised me. I have left everything I own behind ... my house, all my work of the last seven years, my possessions, they're all there for anyone who wants them ... and the government gentlemen will have struck me off their records for deserting my post without leave. But I couldn't live any longer in that house or in that city ... in that world where everything reminded me of her. I fled like a thief in the night, just to escape her, just to forget. But ... as I came on board at night, it was midnight, my friend was with me ... they ... they were just hauling something up by crane, something rectangular and black ... her coffin ... do you hear that, her coffin? She has followed me here, just as I followed her ... and I had to stand by and pretend to be a stranger, because he, her husband, was with it, it's going back to England with him. Perhaps he plans to have an autopsy carried out there ... he has snatched her back, she's his again now, not ours, she no longer belongs to the two of us. But I am still here ... I will go with her to the end ... he will not, must not ever know about it. I will defend her secret against any attempt to ... against this ruffian from whom she fled to her death. He will learn nothing, nothing ... her secret is mine alone ...

So now do you understand ... do you realise why I can't endure the company of human beings? I can't bear their laughter, to hear them flirting and mating ... for her coffin is stowed away down there in the hold, between bales of tea and Brazil nuts. I can't get at it, the hold is locked, but I'm aware of it with all my senses, I know it is there every second of the day ... even if they play waltzes and tangos up here. It's stupid, the sea there washes over millions of dead, a corpse is rotting beneath every plot of ground on which we step … yet I can't bear it, I cannot bear it when they give fancy dress balls and laugh so lasciviously. I feel her dead presence, and I know what she wants. I know it, I still have a duty to do … I'm not finished yet, her secret is not quite safe, she won't let me go yet … "

Slow footsteps and slapping sounds came from amidships; the sailors were beginning to scour the deck. He started as if caught in a guilty act, and his strained face looked anxious. Rising, he murmured, "I'll be off … I'll be off." It was painful to see him: his devastated glance, his swollen eyes, red with drink or tears. He didn't want my pity; I sensed shame in his hunched form, endless shame for giving his story away to me during the night. On impulse, I asked him, "May I visit you in your cabin this afternoon?"

He looked at me—there was a derisive, harsh, sardonic set to his mouth. A touch of malevolence came out with every word, distorting it.

"Ah, your famous duty—the duty to help! I see. You were fortunate enough to make me talk by quoting that maxim. But no thank you, sir. Don't think I feel better now that I have torn my guts out before you, shown you the filth inside me. There's no mending my spoiled life any more … I have served the honourable Dutch government for nothing, I can wave goodbye to my pension—I come back to Europe a poor, penniless cur … a cur whining behind a coffin. You don't run amok for long with impunity, you're bound to be struck down in the end, and I hope it will soon all be over for me. No thank you, sir, I'll turn down your kind offer … I have my own friends in my cabin, a few good bottles of old whisky that sometimes comfort me, and then I have my old friend of the past, although I didn't turn it against myself when I should have done, my faithful Browning. In the end it will help me better than any talk. Please don't try to … the one human right one has left is to die as one wishes, and keep well away from any stranger's help.'

Once more he gave me a derisive, indeed challenging look, but I felt that it was really only in shame, endless shame. Then he hunched his shoulders, turned without a word of farewell and crossed the foredeck, which was already in bright sunlight, making for the cabins and holding himself in that curious way, leaning sideways, footsteps dragging. I never saw him again. I looked for him in our usual place that night, and the next night too. He kept out of sight, and I might have thought he was a dream of mine or a fantastic apparition had I not then noticed, among the passengers, a man with a black mourning band around his arm, a Dutch merchant, I was told, whose wife had just died of some tropical disease. I saw him walking up and down, grave and grieving, keeping away from the others, and the idea that I knew about his secret sorrow made me oddly timid. I always turned aside when he passed by, so as not to give away with so much as a glance that I knew more about his sad story than he did himself.

Then, in Naples harbour, there was that remarkable accident, and I believe I can find its cause in the stranger's story. For most of the passengers had gone ashore that evening—I myself went to the opera, and then to one of the brightly lit cafés on the Via Roma. As we were on our way back to the ship in a dinghy, I noticed several boats circling the vessel with torches and acetylene lamps as if in search of something, and up on the dark deck there was much mysterious coming-and-going of *carabinieri* and of other policemen. I asked a sailor what had happened. He avoided giving a direct answer in a way that immediately told me the crew had orders to keep quiet, and next day too, when all was calm on board again and we sailed on to Genoa without a hint of any further incident, there was nothing to be learned on board. Not until I saw the Italian newspapers did I read accounts, written up in flowery terms, of the alleged accident in Naples harbour. On the night in question, they wrote, at a quiet time in order to avoid upsetting the passengers, the coffin of a distinguished lady from the Dutch colonies was to be moved from the ship to a boat, and it had just been let down the ship's side on a rope ladder in her husband's presence when something heavy fell from the deck above, carrying the coffin away into the sea, along with the men handling it and the woman's husband, who was helping them to hoist it down. One newspaper said that a madman had flung himself down the steps and onto the rope ladder; another stated that the ladder had broken of itself under too much weight. In any case, the shipping company had done all it could to cover up what exactly had happened. The handlers of the coffin and the dead woman's husband had been pulled out of the water and into boats, not without some difficulty, but the lead coffin itself sank straight to the bottom, and could not be retrieved. The brief mention in another report of the fact that, at the same time, the body of a man of about forty had been washed ashore in the harbour did not seem to be connected in the public mind with the romantic account of the accident. But as soon as I had read those few lines, I felt as if that white, moonlit face with its gleaming glasses were staring back at me again, in ghostly fashion, from behind the sheet of newsprint.

THE STAR ABOVE
THE FOREST

A STRANGE THING HAPPENED one day when the slender, elegantly groomed waiter François was leaning over the beautiful Polish Baroness Ostrovska's shoulder to serve her. It lasted for only a second, it was not marked by any start or sudden movement of surprise, any restlessness or momentary agitation. Yet it was one of those seconds in which thousands of hours and days of rejoicing and torment are held spellbound, just as all the wild force of a forest of tall, dark, rustling oak trees, with their rocking branches and swaying crowns, is contained in a single tiny acorn dropping through the air. To outward appearance, nothing happened during that second. With a supple movement François, the waiter in the grand hotel on the Riviera, leaned further down to place the serving platter at a more convenient angle for the Baroness's questing knife. For that one moment, however, his face was just above her softly curling, fragrant waves of hair, and when he instinctively opened the eyes that he had respectfully closed, his reeling gaze saw the gentle white radiance of the line of her neck as it disappeared from that dark cascade of hair, to be lost in her dark red, full-skirted dress. He felt as if crimson flames were flaring up in him. And her knife clinked quietly on the platter, which was imperceptibly shaking. But although in that second he foresaw all the fateful consequences of his sudden enchantment, he expertly mastered his emotion and went on serving at the table with the cool, slightly debonair stylishness of a well-trained waiter with

81

impeccable good taste. He handed the platter calmly to the Baroness's usual companion at table, an elderly aristocrat with gracefully assured manners, who was talking of unimportant matters in crystal-clear French with a very faint accent. Then he walked away from the table without a gesture or a backward glance.

Those minutes were the beginning of his abandoning himself to a very strange kind of devotion, such a reeling, intoxicated sensation that the proud and portentous word 'love' is not quite right for it. It was that faithful, dog-like devotion without desire that those in mid-life seldom feel, and is known only to the very young and the very old. A love devoid of any deliberation, not thinking but only dreaming. He entirely forgot the unjust yet ineradicable disdain that even the clever and considerate show to those who wear a waiter's tailcoat, he did not look for opportunities and chance meetings, but nurtured this strange affection in his blood until its secret fervour was beyond all mockery and criticism. His love was not a matter of secret winks and lurking glances, the sudden boldness of audacious gestures, the senseless ardour of salivating lips and trembling hands; it was quiet toil, the performance of those small services that are all the more sacred and sublime in their humility because they are intended to go unnoticed. After the evening meal he smoothed out the crumpled folds of the tablecloth where she had been sitting with tender, caressing fingers, as one would stroke a beloved woman's soft hands at rest; he adjusted everything close to her with devout symmetry, as if he were preparing it for a special occasion. He carefully carried the glasses that her lips had touched up to his own small, musty attic bedroom, and watched them sparkle like precious jewellery by night when the moonlight streamed in. He was always to be found in some corner, secretly attentive to her as she strolled and walked about. He drank in what she said as you might relish a sweet, fragrantly intoxicating wine on the tongue, and responded to every one of her words and orders as eagerly as children run to catch a ball flying through the air. So his intoxicated soul brought an ever-changing, rich glow into his dull, ordinary life. The wise folly of clothing the whole experience in the cold, destructive words of reality was an idea that never entered his mind: the poor waiter François was in love with an exotic Baroness who would be for ever unattainable. For he did not think of her as reality, but as something very distant, very high above him, sufficient in its mere reflection of life. He loved the imperious pride of her orders, the commanding arch of her black eyebrows that almost touched one another, the wilful lines around her small mouth, the confident grace of her bearing. Subservience seemed to him quite natural, and he felt the humiliating intimacy of menial labour as good fortune, because it enabled him to step so often into the magic circle that surrounded her.

So a dream suddenly awakened in the life of a simple man, like a beautiful, carefully raised garden flower blooming by a roadside where the dust of travel obliterates all other seedlings. It was the frenzy of someone plain and ordinary, an enchanting narcotic dream in the midst of a cold and monotonous life. And such people's dreams are like a rudderless boat drifting aimlessly on quiet, shining waters, rocking with delight, until suddenly its keel grounds abruptly on an unknown bank.

However, reality is stronger and more robust than any dreams. One evening the stout hotel porter from Waadland told him in passing, "Baroness Ostrovska is leaving tomorrow night on the eight o'clock train." And he added a couple of other names which meant nothing to François, and which he did not note. For those words had turned to a confused, tumultuous roaring in his head. A couple of times he mechanically ran his fingers over his aching brow, as if to push away an oppressive weight lying there and dimming his understanding. He took a few steps; he was unsteady on his feet. Alarmed and uncertain, he passed a tall, gilt-framed mirror from which a pale strange face looked back at him, white as a sheet. No ideas would come to him; they seemed to be held captive behind a dark and misty wall. Almost unconsciously, he felt his way down by the hand-rail of the broad flight of steps into the twilit garden, where tall pines stood alone like dark thoughts. His restless figure took a few more shaky steps, like the low reeling flight of a large dark nocturnal bird, and then he sank down on a bench with his head pressed to its cool back. It was perfectly quiet. The sea sparkled here and there beyond the round shapes of shrubs. Faint, trembling lights shone out on the water, and the monotonous, murmuring sing-song of distant breakers was lost in the silence.

Suddenly everything was clear to him, perfectly clear. So painfully clear that he could almost summon up a smile. It was all over. Baroness Ostrovska was going home, and François the waiter would stay at his post. Was that so strange? Didn't all the foreign guests who came to the hotel leave again after two, three or four weeks? How foolish not to have thought of it before. It was so clear, it was enough to make you laugh or cry. And ideas kept whirring through his head. Tomorrow evening on the eight o'clock train to Warsaw. To Warsaw—hours and hours of travel through forests and valleys, passing hills and mountains, steppes and rivers and noisy towns. Warsaw! It was so far away! He couldn't even imagine it, but he felt it in the depths of his heart, that proud and threatening, harsh and distant word Warsaw. While he …

For a second a small, dream-like hope fluttered up in his heart. He could follow. He could hire himself out there as a servant, a secretary, could stand in the street as a freezing beggar, anything not to be so dreadfully far away, just to breathe the air of the same city, perhaps see her sometimes driving past, catch a glimpse of her shadow, her dress, her dark hair. Daydreams flashed hastily through his mind. But this was a hard and pitiless hour. Clear and plain, he saw how unattainable his dreams were. He worked it out: at the most he had savings of a hundred or two hundred francs. That would scarcely take him half the way. And then what? As if through a torn veil he suddenly saw his own life, knew how wretched, pitiful, hateful it must be now. Empty, desolate years working as a waiter, tormented by foolish longing—was something so ridiculous to be his future? The idea made him shudder. And suddenly all these trains of thoughts came stormily and inevitably together. There was only one way out …

The treetops swayed quietly in an imperceptible breeze. A dark, black night menacingly faced him. He rose from his bench, confident and composed, and walked over the crunching gravel up to the great building of the hotel where it slumbered in white silence. He stopped outside her windows. They were dark, with no spark of light at which his dreamy longing could have been kindled. Now his blood was flowing calmly, and he walked like a man whom nothing will ever confuse or deceive again. In his room, he flung himself on the bed without any sign of agitation, and slept a dull, dreamless sleep until the alarm summoned him to get up in the morning.

Next day his demeanour was entirely within the bounds of carefully calculated reflection and self-imposed calm. He carried out his duties with cool indifference, and his gestures were so sure and easy that no one could have guessed at the bitter decision behind his deceptive mask. Just before dinner he hurried out with his small savings to the best florist in the resort and bought choice flowers whose colourful glory spoke to him like words: tulips glowing with fiery, passionate gold—shaggy white chrysanthemums resembling light, exotic dreams—slender orchids, the graceful images of longing—and a few proud, intoxicating roses. And then he bought a magnificent vase of sparkling, opalescent glass. He gave the few francs he still had left to a beggar child in passing, with a quick and carefree movement. Then he hurried back. With sad solemnity, he put the vase of flowers down in front of the Baroness's place at table, which he now prepared for the last time with slow, voluptuously meticulous attention.

Then came the dinner. He served it as usual: cool, silent, skilful, without looking up. Only at the end did he embrace her supple, proud figure with an endlessly long look of which she never knew. And she had never seemed to him so beautiful as in that last, perfect look. Then he stepped calmly back from the table, without any gesture of farewell, and left the dining room. Bearing himself like a guest to whom the staff would bow and nod their heads, he walked down the corridors and the handsome flight of steps outside the reception area and out into the street: any observer must surely have been able to tell that, at that moment, he was leaving his past behind. He stood outside the hotel for a moment, undecided, and then turned to the bright villas and wide gardens, following the road past them, walking on, ever on with his thoughtful, dignified stride, with no idea where he was going.

He wandered restlessly like this until evening, in a lost, dreamy state of mind. He was not thinking of anything any more. Not about the past, or the inevitable moment to come. He was no longer playing with ideas of death, not in the way one might well pick up a shining revolver with its deep, menacing mouth in those last moments, weighing it in the hand, and then lower it again. He had passed sentence on himself long ago. Only images came to him now in rapid flight, like swallows soaring. First images of his youthful days, up to a fateful moment at school when a foolish adventure had suddenly closed an alluring future to him and thrust him out into the turmoil of the world. Then his restless wanderings, his efforts to earn a living, all the attempts that kept failing, until the great black

wave that we call destiny broke his pride and he ended up
in a position unworthy of him. Many colourful memories
whirled past. And finally the gentle reflection of these last
few days glowed in his waking dreams, suddenly pushing
the dark door of reality open again. He had to go through
it. He remembered that he intended to die today.

For a while he thought of the many ways leading to
death, assessing their comparative bitterness and speed,
until suddenly an idea shot through his mind. His clouded senses abruptly showed him a dark symbol: just as she
had unknowingly, destructively driven over his fate, so
she should also crush his body. She herself would do it.
She would finish her own work. And now his ideas came
thick and fast with strange certainty. In just under an
hour, at eight, the express carrying her away from him
left. He would throw himself under its wheels, let himself
be trampled down by the same violent force that was
tearing the woman of his dreams from him. He would
bleed to death beneath her feet. The ideas stormed on
after one another as if in jubilation. He knew the right
place too: further off, near the wooded slope, where the
swaying treetops hid the sight of the last bend in the railway line nearby. He looked at his watch; the seconds and
his hammering blood were beating out the same rhythm.
It was time to set off. Now a spring returned to his sluggish footsteps, along with the certainty of his destination.
He walked at that brisk, hasty pace that does away with
dreaming as one goes forward, restlessly striding on in the
twilight glory of the Mediterranean evening towards the
place where the sky was a streak of purple lying embed-
ded between distant, wooded hills. And he hurried on

until he came to the two silver lines of the railway track shining ahead of him, guiding him on his way. The track led him by winding paths on through the deep, fragrant valleys, their veils of mist now silvered by the soft moonlight, it took him into the hilly landscape where the sight of sparkling lights along the beach showed how far away the nocturnal, black expanse of the sea was now. And at last it presented him with the deep, restlessly whispering forest that hid the railway line in its lowering shadows.

It was late when, breathing heavily, he reached the dark wooded slope. The trees stood around him, black and ominous, but high above, in their shimmering crowns, faint, quivering moonlight was caught in the branches that moaned as they embraced the slight nocturnal breeze. Sometimes this hollow silence was broken by the strange cries of night birds. In this alarming isolation, his thoughts froze entirely. He was merely waiting, waiting and straining his eyes to see the red light of the train appearing down by the curve of the first bend. Sometimes he looked nervously at his watch again, counting seconds. Then he listened once more, thinking that he heard the distant whistle of the locomotive. But it was a false alarm. All was perfectly silent again. Time seemed to stand still.

At last, far away, he saw the light. At that moment he felt a pang in his heart, and could not have said if it was fear or jubilation. He flung himself down on the rails with a brusque movement. At first he felt the pleasantly cool sensation of the strips of iron against his temples for a moment. Then he listened. The train was still far off. It might be several minutes yet. There was nothing to be heard but the whispering of the trees in the wind.

His thoughts went this way and that in confusion, until suddenly one stopped and pierced his heart painfully, like an arrow: he was dying for her sake, and she would never know. Not a single gentle ripple of his life as it came to its turbulent end had ever touched hers. She would never know that a stranger's life had depended on her own, and had been crushed by it.

Very quietly, the rhythmic chugging of the approaching engine came through the breathless air from afar. But that idea burned on, tormenting the dying man in his last minutes. The train rattled closer and closer. Then he opened his eyes once more. Above him was a silent, blue-black sky, with the tops of a few trees swaying in front of it. And above the forest stood a shining, white star. A single star above the forest … the rails beneath his head were already beginning to vibrate and sing faintly. But the idea burned on like fire in his heart, and in his eyes as they saw all the fire and despair of his love. His whole longing and that last painful question flowed into the white and shining star that looked mildly down on him. Closer and closer thundered the train. And once more, with a last inexpressible look, the dying man took the sparkling star above the forest to his heart. Then he closed his eyes. The rails were trembling and swaying, closer and closer came the rattling of the express train, making the forest echo as if great bells were hammering out a rhythm. The earth seemed to sway. One more deafening, rushing, whirring sound, a whirlwind of noise, then a shrill scream, the terrifyingly animal scream of the steam whistle, and the screech and groan of brakes applied in vain …

The beautiful Baroness Ostrovska had a reserved compartment to herself in the express. She had been reading a French magazine since the train left, gently cradled by the rocking movement of the carriage. The air in the enclosed space was sultry, and drenched with the heavy fragrance of many fading flowers. Clusters of white lilac were already hanging heavily, like over-ripe fruit, from the magnificent farewell baskets that she had been given, flowers hung limp on their stems, and the broad, heavy cups of the roses seemed to be withering in the hot cloud of intoxicating perfumes. Even in the haste of the express as it rushed along, a suffocatingly close atmosphere heated the heavy drifts of perfume weighing oppressively down.

Suddenly she lowered her book with limp fingers. She herself did not know why. Some secret feeling was tearing at her. She felt a dull but painful pressure. A sudden sense of constriction that she couldn't explain clutched her heart. She thought she would choke on the heavy, intoxicating aroma of the flowers. And that terrifying pain did not pass, she felt every revolution of the rushing wheels, their blind, pounding, forward movement was an unspeakable torment. Suddenly she longed to be able to halt the swift momentum of the train, to haul it back from the dark pain towards which it was racing. She had never in her life felt such fear of something terrible, invisible and cruel seizing on her heart as she did now, in those seconds of incomprehensible, incredible pain and fear. And that unspeakable feeling grew stronger and stronger, tightening its grasp around her throat. The idea of being able to stop the train was like a prayer moaned out loud in her mind …

Then she hears a sudden shrill whistle, the wild, warning scream of the locomotive, the wailing groan and crunch of the brakes. And the rhythm of the flying wheels slackens, goes slower and slower, until there is a stuttering rattle and a faltering jerk.

With difficulty, she makes her way to the window to fill her lungs with fresh air. The pane rattles down. Dark figures are hurrying around ... words fly back and forth, different voices: a suicide ... under the wheels ... dead ... yes, out here in the open ...

She starts. Instinctively, her eyes go to the high and silent sky and the dark trees whispering above it. And beyond them, a single star is shining over the forest. She is aware of its gaze on her like a sparkling tear. Looking at it, she abruptly feels such grief as she has never known before. A fiery grief, full of a longing that has not been part of her own life ...

Slowly, the train rattles on. She leans back in the corner and feels soft tears running down over her cheeks. That dull fear has gone away, she feels only a deep, strange pain, and seeks in vain to discover its source. A pain such as terrified children feel when they suddenly wake on a dark, impenetrable night, and feel that they are all alone ...

LEPORELLA

HER REAL NAME WAS Crescentia Anna Aloisia Finken-huber, she was thirty-nine years old, she had been born out of wedlock and came from a small mountain village in the Ziller valley. Under the heading of 'Distinguishing Marks' in the booklet recording her employment as a servant, a single line scored across the space available signified that she had none, but if the authorities had been obliged to give a description of her character, the most fleeting glance would have required a remark there, reading: resembles a hard-driven, strong-boned, scrawny mountain horse. For there was something unmistakably horsy about the expression of her heavy, drooping lower lip, the oval of her sun-tanned face, which was both long and harshly outlined, her dull, lashless gaze, and in particular the thick, felted strands of hair that fell greasily over her brow. Even the way she moved suggested the obstinacy and stubborn, mule-like manner of a horse used to the Alpine passes, carrying the same wooden panniers dourly uphill and downhill along stony bridleways in summer and winter alike. Once released from the halter of her work, Crescenz would doze with her bony hands loosely clasped and her elbows splayed, much as animals stand in the stable, and her senses seemed to be withdrawn. Everything about her was hard, wooden, heavy. She thought laboriously and was slow to understand anything: new ideas penetrated her innermost mind only with difficulty, as if dripping through a close-meshed sieve. But once she

95

had finally taken in some new notion, she clung to it tena-
ciously and jealously. She read neither newspapers nor the
prayer-book, she found writing difficult, and the clumsy
characters in her kitchen records were curiously like her
own heavy but angular figure, which was visibly devoid
of all tangible marks of femininity. Like her bones, her
brow, her hips and hands, her voice was hard too, and in
spite of its thick, throaty Tyrolean accent, always sounded
rusty—which was hardly surprising, since Crescenz never
said an unnecessary word to anyone. And no one had ever
seen her laugh. Here too she was just like an animal, for the
gift of laughter, that release of feeling so happily breaking
out, has not been granted to God's brute creation, which
is perhaps a more cruel deprivation than the lack of language.

Brought up at the expense of the parish because of
her illegitimate birth, put out to domestic service at the
age of twelve, and then later a scullery maid in a carters'
tavern, she had finally left that establishment, where she
was known for her tenacious, ox-like capacity for work,
and had risen to be cook at an inn that was popular with
tourists. Crescenz rose there at five in the morning every
day, worked, swept, cleaned, lit fires, brushed, cleared up,
cooked, kneaded dough, strained food, washed dishes
and did the laundry until late at night. She never took
any holiday, she never went out in the street except to go
to church; the fire in the kitchen range was her sun, the
thousands and thousands of wooden logs it burned over
the years her forest.

Men left her alone, whether because a quarter-century
of dour, dull toil had taken every sign of femininity from

her, or because she had firmly and taciturnly rejected all advances. Her one pleasure was in money, which she doggedly collected with the hamster-like instincts of the rustic labouring class, so that in her old age she would not have to eat the bitter bread of charity in the parish poorhouse yet again.

It was only for the money, in fact, that this dull-witted creature first left her native Tyrol at the age of thirty-seven. A woman who was a professional agent for domestic staff had come there on holiday, saw her working like a madwoman from morning to night in the kitchen and public rooms of the inn, and lured her to Vienna with the promise of a position at double the wages. During the railway journey Crescenz hardly said a word to anyone, and in spite of the friendly offers of other passengers to put the heavy wicker basket containing all her worldly goods up in the net of the luggage rack, she held it on her knees, which were already aching, for deception and theft were the only notions that her clumsy peasant brain connected with the idea of the big city. In her new place in Vienna, she had to be accompanied to market for the first few days, because she feared all the vehicles as a cow fears a motor car. But as soon as she knew her way down the four streets leading to the market place she no longer needed anyone, but trotted off with her basket, never looking up, from the door of the building where her employers lived to the market stalls and home again to sweep the apartment, light fires and clear out her new kitchen range just as she had cleared the old one, noticing no change. She kept rustic hours, went to bed at nine and slept with her mouth open, like an animal, until the alarm clock went off in the morning. No one knew if she liked her job; perhaps she didn't know herself, for she approached no one, answered questions merely with a dull "Very well", or if she didn't agree, with a discontented shrug of her shoulders. She ignored her neighbours and the other maids in the building; the mocking looks of her more light-hearted companions in domestic service slipped off the leathery surface of her indifference like water. Just once, when a girl imitated her Tyrolean dialect and wouldn't stop teasing her for her taciturnity, she suddenly snatched a burning piece of wood out of the range and went for the horrified, screaming young woman with it. From that day on, everyone avoided her, and no one dared to mock someone capable of such fury again.

But every Sunday morning Crescenz went to church in her wide, pleated skirt and flat peasant hat. Only once, on her first day off in Vienna, did she try taking a walk. As she didn't want to ride on the tram, and had seen nothing but more and more stone walls in her cautious exploration of the many bewildering streets, she went only as far as the Danube Canal, where she stared at the flowing water as at something familiar, turned and went back the way she had come, always keeping close to the buildings and anxiously avoiding the carriageway. This first and only expedition must obviously have disappointed her, for after that she never left the house again, but preferred to sit at the window on Sundays either busy with her needlework or empty-handed. So the great metropolis brought no change into the routine treadmill of her days, except that at the end of every month she held four blue banknotes instead of the old two in her gnarled, tough, battered hands. She always checked these banknotes suspiciously for a long time. She unfolded the new notes ceremoniously, and finally smoothed them out flat, almost tenderly, before putting them with the others in the carved, yellow wooden box that she had brought from her home village. This clumsy, heavy little casket was her whole secret, the meaning of her life. By night she put its key under her pillow. No one ever found out where she kept it in the day.

Such was the nature of this strange human being (as we may call her, although humanity was apparent in her behaviour only in a very faint and muted way), but perhaps it took someone with exactly those blinkered senses to tolerate domestic service in the household of young Baron von F—which was an extremely strange one in itself. Most servants couldn't put up with the quarrelsome atmosphere for any longer than the legally binding time between their engagement and the day when they gave notice. The irate shouting, wound up to hysterical pitch, came from the lady of the house. The only daughter of an extremely rich manufacturer in Essen, and no longer in her first youth, she had been at a spa where she met the considerably younger Baron (whose nobility was suspect, while his financial situation was even more dubious), and had quickly married that handsome young ne'er-do-well, ready and able as he was to display aristocratic charm. But as soon as the honeymoon was over, the newly-wedded wife had to admit that her parents, who set great store by solid worth and ability, had been right to oppose the hasty marriage. For it quickly transpired that besides having many debts to which he had not admitted, her husband, whose attentions

to her had soon worn off, showed a good deal more interest in continuing the habits of his bachelor days than in
his marital duties. Although not exactly unkind by nature,
since at heart he was as sunny as light-minded people usually are, but extremely lax and unscrupulous in his general
outlook, that handsome would-be cavalier despised all calculations of interest and capital, considering them stingy,
narrow-minded evidence of plebeian bigotry. He wanted
an easy life; she wanted a well-ordered, respectable domestic existence of the bourgeois Rhineland kind, which got
on his nerves. And when, in spite of her wealth, he had to
haggle to lay hands on any large sum of money, and his
wife, who had a turn for mathematics, even denied him his
dearest wish, a racing stables of his own, he saw no more
reason to involve himself any further in conjugal relations
with the massive, thick-necked North German woman
whose loud and domineering voice fell unpleasantly on
his ears. So he put her on ice, as they say, and without any
harsh gestures, but none the less unmistakably, he kept his
disappointed wife at a distance. If she reproached him
he would listen politely, with apparent compassion, but
as soon as her sermon was over he would wave her passionate admonitions away like the smoke of his cigarette,
and had no qualms about continuing to do exactly as he
pleased. This smooth, almost formal amiability embittered
the disappointed woman more than any opposition. And
as she was completely powerless to do anything about
his well-bred, never abusive and positively overpowering
civility, her pent-up anger broke out violently in a different direction: she ranted and raged at the domestic staff,
wildly venting on the innocent her indignation, which

was fundamentally justified but in those quarters inappropriately expressed. Of course there were consequences: within two years she had been obliged to engage a new lady's maid no less than sixteen times, once after an actual physical scuffle—a considerable sum of money had to be paid in compensation to hush it up.

Only Crescenz stood unmoved, like a patient cab-horse in the rain, in the midst of this stormy tumult. She took no one's side, ignored all changes, didn't seem to notice the arrival of strangers with whom she shared the maids' bedroom and whose names, hair-colour, body-odour and behaviour were constantly different. For she herself talked to no one, didn't mind the slammed doors, the interrupted mealtimes, the helpless and hysterical outbursts. Indifferent to it all, she went busily from her kitchen to market, from market back to her kitchen, and what went on outside that enclosed circle did not concern her. Hard and emotionless as a flail, she dealt with day after day, and so two years in the big city passed her by without incident, never enlarging her inner world, except that the stack of blue banknotes in her little box rose an inch higher, and when she counted the notes one by one with a moistened finger at the end of the year, the magic figure of one thousand wasn't far off.

But Chance works with diamond drills, and that dangerously cunning entity Fate can often intervene from an unexpected quarter, shattering even the rockiest nature entirely. In Crescenz's case, the outward occasion was almost as ordinary as was she herself; after ten years, it pleased the state to hold a new census, and highly complicated forms were sent to all residential buildings to be filled in by their occupants, in detail. Distrusting the illegible handwriting and purely phonetic spelling of his domestic staff, the Baron decided to fill in the forms himself, and to this end he summoned Crescenz to his study. When he asked for her name, age and date of birth, it turned out that as a passionate huntsman and a friend of the owner of the local game preserves, he had often shot chamois in that very corner of the Alps from which Crescenz came. A guide from her native village had actually been his companion for two weeks. And when, extraordinarily, it turned out that this same guide was Crescenz's uncle, the chance discovery led on the Baron, who was in a cheerful mood, to further conversation, in the course of which another surprising fact came to light: on his visit to the area, he had eaten an excellent dish of roast venison at the very same inn where she was cook. None of this was of any importance, but the power of coincidence made it seem strange, and to Crescenz, for the first time meeting someone who knew her home here in Vienna, it appeared miraculous. She stood before him with a flushed, interested face, bobbed clumsily, felt flattered when he went on to crack some jokes, imitating the Tyrolean dialect and asking if she could yodel, and talked similar schoolboy nonsense. Finally, amused at himself, he slapped her hard behind with the palm of his hand in the friendly peasant way and dismissed her with a laugh. "Off you go then, my good Cenzi, and here's two crowns because you're from the Ziller valley."

In itself this was not a significant emotional event, to be sure. But that five minutes of conversation had an effect on the fish-like, underground currents of Crescenz's dull nature like that of a stone being dropped into a swamp: ripples form, lethargically and gradually at first, but moving sluggishly on until they slowly reach the edge of consciousness. For the first time in years, the obdurate and taciturn Crescenz had held a personal conversation with another human being, and it seemed to her a super-natural dispensation of Providence that this first person to have spoken to her in the midst of the stony maze of the city knew her own mountains, and had even once eaten roast venison that she herself had prepared. And then there was that casual slap on the behind, which in peasant language represents a kind of laconic courtship of a woman. Although Crescenz did not make so bold as to suppose that such an elegant and distinguished gentle-man had actually been expressing any intentions of that sort towards herself, the physical familiarity somehow shook her slumbering senses awake.

So that chance impetus set off movement in the under-ground realm within her, shifting stratum after stratum, until at last, first clumsily and then ever more clearly, a new feeling developed in her, like that sudden moment when one day a dog unexpectedly recognises one of the many two-legged figures around him as his master. From that hour on the dog follows him, greets the man whom Fate has set in authority over him by wagging his tail or barking, becomes voluntarily subservient and follows his trail obediently step by step. In just the same way, some-thing new had entered the small circle of Crescenz's life, hitherto bounded by the five familiar ideas of money, the market, the kitchen range, church and her bed. That new element needed space, and brusquely pushed everything else forcefully aside. And with that peasant greed that will never let something it has seized out of its hands again, she drew it deep into herself and the confused, instinctive world of her dull senses. Of course it was some time before any change became visible, and those first signs were very insignificant: for instance, the particularly fanatical care she devoted to cleaning the Baron's clothes and shoes, while she still left the Baroness's to the lady's maid. Or she was often to be seen in the corridor of the apartment, eagerly making haste to take his hat and stick as soon as she heard the sound of the key in the front door. She redoubled her attention to the cooking, and even laboriously made her way to the big market hall so that she could get a joint of venison to roast specially for him. She was taking more care with her outward appearance too.

It was one or two weeks before these first shoots of new emotion emerged from her inner world, and many weeks more before a second idea was added to the first and grew, uncertainly in the beginning, but then acquiring distinct form and colour. This new feeling was complementary to the first: initially indistinct, but gradually appearing clear and plain, it was a sense of emergent hatred for the Baron's wife, the woman who could live with him, sleep with him, talk to him, yet did not feel the same devoted veneration for him as she herself did. Whether because she had perhaps—these days instinctively noticing more—witnessed one of those shameful scenes in which the master she idolized was humiliated in the most objectionable way by his irate wife, or whether it was that the inhibited North German woman's arrogant reserve was doubly obvious

in contrast to his jovial familiarity—for one reason or
another, at any rate, she suddenly brought a certain mul-
ishness to bear on the unsuspecting wife, a prickly hostility
expressed in a thousand little barbed remarks and spiteful
actions. For instance, the Baroness always had to ring at
least twice before Crescenz responded to the summons,
deliberately slowly and with obvious reluctance, and her
hunched shoulders always expressed resistance in princi-
ple. She accepted orders and errands wordlessly and with
a glum expression, so that the Baroness never knew if she
had actually understood her, but if she asked again to be
on the safe side she got only a gloomy nod or a derisive
"Sure I hears yer!" by way of answer. Or just before a visit
to the theatre, while the Baroness was nervously scurrying
around, an important key would prove to be lost, only to
be unexpectedly discovered in a corner half-an-hour later.
She regularly chose to forget about messages and phone
calls to the Baroness: when charged with the omission
she would offer, without the slightest sign of regret, only
a brusque, "I fergot 'un". She never looked the Baroness
in the face, perhaps for fear that she would not be able to
hide her hatred.

Meanwhile the domestic differences between husband
and wife led to increasingly unedifying scenes; perhaps
Crescenz's unconsciously provocative surliness also had
something to do with the hot temper of the Baroness,
who was becoming more overwrought every week. With
her nerves unstable as a result of preserving her virginity
too long, and embittered by her husband's indifference,
the exasperated woman was losing control of herself. In
vain did she try to soothe her agitation with bromide and

veronal; the tension of her overstretched nerves showed all the more violently in arguments, she had fits of weeping and hysteria, and never received the slightest sympathy or even the appearance of kindly support from anyone at all. Finally the doctor who had been called in recommended a two-month stay in a sanatorium, a proposal that was approved by her usually indifferent husband with such sudden concern for her health that his wife, suspicious again, at first balked at the idea. But in the end it was decided that she would take the trip, with her lady's maid to accompany her, while Crescenz was to stay behind in the spacious apartment to serve her master.

The news that her master was to be entrusted to her care alone affected Crescenz's dull senses like a sudden tonic. As if all her strength and zest for life had been shaken wildly up in a magic flask, a hidden sediment of passion now rose from the depths of her being and lent its colour to her whole conduct. The sluggish heaviness suddenly left her rigid, frozen limbs; it was as if since she had heard that electrifying news her joints were suddenly supple, and she adopted a quick, nimble gait. She ran back and forth between the rooms, up and down the stairs, when it was time to make preparations for the journey she packed all the cases, unasked, and carried them to the car herself. And then, when the Baron came back from the railway station late in the evening, and handed her his stick and coat as she eagerly came to his aid, saying with a sigh of relief, "She's on her way!" something strange happened. All at once a powerful stretching movement became visible around Crescenz's narrowed lips, although in the normal way, like all animals, she never laughed. Now her mouth twisted, became a wide horizontal line, and suddenly a grin appeared in the middle of her idiotically brightening face. It displayed such frank, animal lack of inhibition that the Baron, embarrassed and surprised by the sight, was ashamed of his inappropriate familiarity with the servant, and disappeared into his study without a word.

But that fleeting second of discomfort quickly passed over, and during the next few days the two of them, master and maid, were united in their sense of shared relief, enjoying the precious silence and independence that did them both good. The departure of the Baron's wife had lifted a lowering cloud, so to speak, from the atmosphere; the liberated husband, happily freed from the constant necessity to account for himself, came late home that very first evening, and the silent attentions of Crescenz were an agreeable contrast to his wife's only too voluble reception of him. Crescenz flung herself into her daily work again with passionate enthusiasm, rose particularly early, scoured everything until it shone, polished doorknobs and handles like a woman possessed, conjured up particularly delicious menus, and to his surprise the Baron noticed, when she first served him lunch, that the valuable china and cutlery kept in the silver cupboard except on special occasions had been taken out just for him. Not an observant man in general, he couldn't help noticing the attentive, almost affectionate care that this strange creature was taking, and kindly as he was at heart, he expressed his satisfaction freely. He praised her cooking, gave her a few friendly words, and when next morning, which happened to be his name-day, he found that she had made an elaborate cake with his initials and coat of arms on it in sugar icing, he smiled at her in high spirits. "You really are spoiling me, Cenzi! And what am I to do when—heaven forbid!—my wife comes home again?"

All the same, he kept a certain control over himself for a few days before casting off the last of his scruples. But then, feeling sure from various signs that she would keep silent, he began living the bachelor life again, making himself comfortable in his own apartment. On his fourth day as a grass widower he summoned Crescenz and told her, without further explanation, that he would like her to prepare a cold supper for two that evening and then go to bed; he would see to everything else himself. Crescenz received the order in silence. Not a glance, not the faintest look showed whether the real purport of what he said had penetrated her low forehead. But her master soon saw, with surprised amusement, how well she understood his real intentions, for when he came home from the theatre late that evening with a little music student who was studying opera, not only did he find the table beautifully laid and decorated with flowers, but the bed next to his own in the bedroom was invitingly if brazenly turned down, and his wife's silk dressing gown and slippers were laid out ready. The liberated husband instinctively smiled at the far-sighted thoughtfulness of that strange creature Crescenz. And with that he threw off the last of his inhibitions about letting the helpful soul into his confidence. He rang next morning for her to help the amorous intruder get dressed, and that finally sealed the silent agreement between them.

It was in those days, too, that Crescenz acquired her new name. The merry little music student, who was studying the part of Donna Elvira and in jest liked to elevate her lover to the role of Don Giovanni, had once said to him, laughing, "Now, do call for your Leporella!" The name amused him, just because it was so grotesque a parody when applied to the gaunt Tyrolean woman, and from now on he never called her anything but Leporella. Crescenz, who looked up in surprise the first time but was then enchanted by the pleasing vocal music of her new name, which she did not understand in the least, regarded it as a sign of distinction; whenever her high-spirited master called for her by that name her thin lips would part, exposing her brown, horse-like teeth, and like a dog wagging its tail, she submissively hurried to receive her lord and master's orders.

The name was intended as a joke, but the budding operatic diva had unintentionally hit the mark, throwing her a verbal dress that magically suited her. For like Don Giovanni's appreciative accomplice as depicted by Da Ponte, this bony old maid who had never known love took a curious pride and pleasure in her master's adventures. Was it just her satisfaction at seeing the bed of the wife she hated so much tumbled and desecrated every morning by now one, now another young body, or did a secret sense of conspiratorial pleasure make her own senses tingle? In any case, the stern, narrow-minded spinster showed a positively passionate readiness to be of service to her master in all his adventures. It was a long time since her own hard-worked body, now sexless after decades of labour, had felt any such urges, but she warmed herself

comfortably, like a procuress, on the satisfaction of seeing a second young woman in the bedroom after a few
days, and then a third; her share in the conspiracy and
the exciting perfume of the erotic atmosphere worked
like a stimulant on her dulled senses. Crescenz really
did become Leporella, and was nimble, alert and ready
to jump to attention; strange qualities appeared in her
nature, as if forced into being by the flowing heat of her
burning interest, all kinds of little tricks, touches of mis-
chief, sharp remarks, a curiosity that made her eavesdrop
and lurk in waiting. She was almost frolicking. She listened at doors, looked through keyholes, searched rooms
and beds, flew upstairs and downstairs in excitement as
soon as, like a huntswoman, she scented new prey; and
gradually this alertness, this curious, interested sympathy
reshaped the wooden shell of her old dull lethargy into
some kind of living human being. To the general astonishment of the neighbours, Crescenz suddenly became
sociable, she chatted to the maids in the building, cracked
broad jokes with the postman, began chatting and gossip-
ing with the women at the market stalls, and once in the
evening, when the lights in the courtyard were out, the
maidservants sleeping in the building in a room opposite
hers heard a strange humming sound at the usually silent
window: awkwardly, in a muted, rusty voice, Crescenz
was singing one of those Alpine songs that herdswomen
sing on the pastures at evening. The monotonous melody
staggered out of her unpractised lips with difficulty, in a
cracked tone, but it did come out, a strange and gripping
sound. Crescenz was trying to sing again for the first time
since her childhood, and there was something touching in

those stumbling notes that rose with difficulty to the light out of the darkness of buried years.

The unconscious author of this change in the woman who was so devoted to him, the Baron, noticed it less than anyone, for who ever turns to look at his own shadow? He knows it is following faithfully and silently along behind his own footsteps, sometimes hurrying ahead like a wish of which he is not yet conscious, but he seldom tries to observe its shape imitating his, or to recognise himself in its distortion. The Baron noticed nothing about Crescenz except that she was always there at his service, perfectly silent, reliable and devoted to him to the point of self-abnegation. And he felt that her very silence, the distance she naturally preserved in all discreet situations, was specially beneficial; sometimes he casually gave her a few words of appreciation, as one might pat a dog, now and then he even joked with her, pinched her earlobe in kindly fashion, gave her a banknote or a theatre ticket—small things for him, taken from his waistcoat pocket without a moment's thought, but to her they were holy relics to be treasured in her little wooden box. Gradually he had become accustomed to thinking out loud in front of her, and even entrusting complex errands to her—and the greater the signs he gave of his confidence in her, the more gratefully and assiduously did she exert herself. An odd sniffing, searching, tracking instinct gradually appeared in her as she tried to spy out his wishes and even anticipate them; her whole life, all she did and all she wished for, seemed to pass from her own body into his; she saw everything with his eyes, listened hard to guess what he was feeling, and with almost depraved enthusiasm shared his enjoyment of all his pleasures and conquests. She beamed when a new young woman crossed the threshold, and looked downcast, as if her expectations were disappointed, if he came home at night without such amorous company—her once sluggish mind was now working as quickly and restlessly as only her hands used to, and a new, vigilant light shone in her eyes. A human being had awoken in the tired, worn-out work-horse—a human being who was reserved and sombre but cunning and dangerous, thinking and then acting on her thoughts, restless and intriguing.

Once when the Baron came home unexpectedly early, he stopped in the corridor in surprise: wasn't that giggling and laughter behind the usually silent kitchen door? And then Leporella appeared in the doorway, rubbing her hands on her apron, bold and awkward at the same time. "'Scuse us, sir," she said, eyes on the floor, "it's the pastry-cook's daughter's here, a pretty girl she be, she'd like to meet sir ever so!" The Baron looked up in surprise, not sure whether he should be angry at such outrageous familiarity or amused at her readiness to procure for him. Finally his male curiosity won the day. "Well, let her have a look at me!"

The girl, a fresh, blond sixteen-year-old, whom Leporella had gradually enticed with flattering talk, appeared, blushing, and with an embarrassed giggle as the maid firmly pushed her through the doorway, and twirled clumsily in front of the elegant gentleman, whom she had indeed often watched with half-childlike admiration from the pâtisserie opposite. The Baron thought her pretty, and invited her to take a cup of tea in his study. Uncertain whether she ought to accept, the girl turned to look for Crescenz, but she had already disappeared into the kitchen with conspicuous haste, so there was nothing the girl could do, having been lured into this adventure, but accept the dangerous invitation, flushed and excited with curiosity.

But nature cannot leap too far: though the pressure of a distorted, confused passion might have aroused a certain mental agility in her dull and angular nature, Crescenz's newly acquired and limited powers of thought were not enough to overcome the next obstacle. In that, they were still related to an animal's short-term instincts. Immured in her obsession to serve the master she loved with dog-like devotion in every way, Crescenz entirely forgot his absent wife. Her awakening was all the more terrible: it was like thunder coming out of a clear sky when one morning the Baron came in with a letter in his hand, looking annoyed, and brusquely told her to set every-thing in the apartment to rights, because his wife was coming home from the sanatorium next day. Crescenz stood there pale-faced, her mouth open with the shock: the news had struck her like a knife. She just stared and stared, as if she didn't understand. And so immeasur-ably and alarmingly did this thunderclap distort her face that the Baron thought he should calm her a little with a light-hearted comment. "It looks to me as if you're not best pleased either, Cenzi, but there's nothing anyone can do about it."

Soon, however, something began to move in her rigid face again. It worked its way up from deep down in her, as if coming out of her guts, a mighty convulsion that gradually brought dark red colour to the cheeks that had been white just now. Very slowly, forced out with harsh thrusts like heartbeats, words emerged: her throat was trembling under the pressure of the effort. And at last they were there and came dully through her gritted teeth. "Could be—could be summat as 'un could do … "

It had come out harsh as the firing of a deadly shot. And so evil, so darkly determined did that distorted face look after she had vented her feelings with such violence that the Baron instinctively started, flinching back in surprise. But Crescenz had already turned away again, and was beginning to scour a copper bowl with such convulsive zeal that she looked as if she meant to break her fingers on it.

With the home-coming of the Baron's wife, stormy winds filled the apartment again, slamming doors, blowing angrily through the rooms, sweeping away the comfortable, warm atmosphere like a cold draught. Whether the deceived wife had found out, from informers among the neighbours or anonymous letters, about the despicable way in which her husband had abused the freedom of the household, or whether the nervous and obvious ill temper that he did not scruple to show on her return had upset her, no one could tell—but in any case, two months in the sanatorium seemed to have done her strained nerves no good, for weeping fits now alternated with occasional threats and hysterical scenes. Relations between the couple became more insufferable every day. For a few weeks the Baron manfully defied the storm of her reproaches with the civility he had always preserved before, and replied evasively and indirectly when she threatened him with divorce or letters to her parents. But this cool, loveless indifference of his in itself drove the friendless woman, surrounded as she was by secret hostility, further and further into her nervous agitation.

Crescenz had armoured herself entirely in her old silence. But that silence had turned aggressive and dangerous. On her mistress's arrival she defiantly stayed in the kitchen, and when she was finally summoned she avoided wishing the Baroness well on her return. Shoulders obdurately braced, she stood there like a block of wood and replied with such surliness to all questions that her impatient mistress soon turned away from her. With one glance, however, Crescenz darted all her pent-up hatred at the unsuspecting woman's back. Her greedy emotions felt wrongfully robbed by the Baroness's return; from the delights of the service she had so passionately relished, she was thrust back into the kitchen and the range, deprived of her intimate name of Leporella. For the Baron carefully avoided showing any liking for Crescenz in front of his wife. Sometimes, however, when he was exhausted by the unendurable scenes, and feeling in need of comfort and wanted to vent his feelings, he would slip into the kitchen and sit down on one of the hard wooden chairs, just so that he could groan, "I can't stand this any longer!"

These moments, when the master she idolized sought refuge with her from his excessive tension, were the happiest of Leporella's life. She never ventured to reply or say a word of consolation; silent and lost in thought, she just sat there, and only looked up sometimes with a sympathetic, receptive and tormented glance at her god, thus humiliated. Her silent sympathy did him good. But once he had left the kitchen, an angry fold would return to her brow, and her heavy hands expressed her anger by battering defenceless pieces of meat or savagely scouring dishes and cutlery.

At last the ominous atmosphere in the apartment since the wife's return discharged itself stormily; during one of the couple's intemperate scenes the Baron finally lost patience, abruptly abandoned the meekly indifferent schoolboy attitude he had adopted, and slammed the door behind him. "I've had enough of this," he shouted so angrily that all the windows in the apartment shook. And still in a furious temper, red in the face, he went out to the kitchen, where Crescenz was quivering like a bent bow. "Pack my case at once and find my sporting gun. I'm going hunting for a week. Even the Devil couldn't endure this hell any more. There has to be an end to it."

Crescenz looked at him happily: like this, he was master in his own house again! And a hoarse laugh emerged from her throat. "Sir be right, there have to be an end to 'un." And twitching with eager zeal, racing from room to room, she hastily snatched everything he would need from cupboards and tables, every nerve of the heavily built creature straining with tension and avidity. She carried the case and the gun out to the car herself. But when he was seeking words to thank her for her eager help, his eyes looked away from her in alarm. For that spiteful smile, the one that always alarmed him, had returned to her narrowed lips. When he saw her seeming to lie in ambush like that, he was instinctively reminded of the low crouching movement of an animal gathering itself to spring. But then she retreated into herself again, and

116

just whispered hoarsely, with almost insulting familiarity, "I hopes sir has a good journey, I'll do 'un all."

Three days later the Baron was called back from his hunting trip by an urgent telegram. His cousin was waiting for him at the railway station. At his very first glance the anxious man knew that something terrible must have happened, for his cousin looked nervous and was fidgeting. After a few words solicitously designed to prepare him, he discovered what it was: his wife had been found dead in her bed that morning, with the whole room full of gas. Unfortunately a careless mistake was out of the question, said his cousin, because now, in May, the gas stove had not been lit for a long time, and his wife's suicidal frame of mind was also obvious from the fact that the unhappy woman had taken some veronal the evening before. In addition there was the statement made by the cook Crescenz, who had been alone at home that evening, and had heard her unfortunate mistress going into the room just outside the bedroom in the night, presumably on purpose to switch on the gas supply, which had been carefully turned off. On hearing this, the police doctor who had also been called in agreed that an accident was out of the question, and recorded death by suicide.

The Baron began to tremble. When his cousin mentioned the statement that Crescenz had made he suddenly felt the blood in his hands turn cold. An unpleasant, a dreadful idea rose in his mind like nausea. But he forcibly suppressed this seething, agonising sensation, and meekly let his cousin take him home. The body had already been removed; family members were waiting in the drawing room with gloomy and hostile expressions. Their condolences were cold as a knife. With a certain accusatory emphasis, they said they thought they should mention that, unfortunately, it had been impossible to hush up the 'scandal', because the maid had rushed out on the stairs that morning screaming, "The mistress has killed herself!" And they had decided on a quiet funeral—yet again that sharp, chilly blade was turned against him—because, deplorably, all kinds of rumours had aroused the curiosity of society to an unwelcome degree. The downcast Baron listened in confusion, and once instinctively raised his eyes to the closed bedroom door, but then cravenly looked away again. He wanted to think something out to the end, an unwelcome idea that kept surfacing in his mind, but all this empty, malicious talk bewildered him. The black-clad relations stood around talking for another half-hour, and then one by one they took their leave. He was left alone in the empty, dimly lit room, trembling as if he had suffered a heavy blow, with an aching head and weariness in his joints.

Then there came a knock at the door. "Come in," he said, rousing himself with a start. And along came a hesitant step, a dragging, stealthy step that he knew well. Suddenly horror overcame him; he felt as if his cervical vertebra were firmly screwed in place, while at the same time the skin from his temples to his knees was rippling with icy shudders. He wanted to turn, but his muscles failed him. So he stood there in the middle of the room, trembling and making no sound, his hands dropping by his sides and rigid as stone, and he felt very clearly how cowardly this guilt-ridden attitude must look. But it was useless for him to exert all his strength: his muscles just would not obey him. The voice behind him said, "I just wants ter ask, sir, will sir eat at home or out?" The Baron shivered ever more violently, and now the icy cold made its way right into his breast. He tried three times before he finally managed to get out the words, "No, I don't want anything to eat." Then the footsteps dragged themselves away, and still he didn't have the courage to turn. And suddenly the rigidity left him: he was shaking all over with spasms, or nausea. He suddenly flung himself at the door and turned the key in it, so that those dreadful footsteps following him like a ghost couldn't get at him. Then he dropped into a chair to force down an idea that he didn't want to entertain, although it kept creeping back into his mind, as cold and slimy as a snail. And this obsessive idea, though he hated the thought of coming close to it, filled all his emotions: it was inescapable, slimy, horrible, and it stayed with him all that sleepless night and during the hours that followed, even when, black-clad and silent, he stood at the head of the coffin during the funeral.

On the day after the funeral the Baron left the city in a hurry. All the faces he saw were too unendurable now: in the midst of their sympathy they had—or was he only imagining it?—a curiously observant, a painfully inquisitorial look. And even inanimate objects spoke to him accusingly, with hostility: every piece of furniture in the apartment, but more particularly in the bedroom where the sweetish smell of gas still seemed to cling to everything, turned him away if he so much as automatically opened the doors. But the really unbearable nightmare of his sleeping and waking hours was the cold, unconcerned indifference of his former accomplice, who went about the empty apartment as if nothing at all had happened. Since that moment at the station when his cousin mentioned her name, he had trembled at the thought of any meeting with her. As soon as he heard her footsteps a nervous, hasty restlessness took hold of him; he couldn't look at that dragging, indifferent gait any more, couldn't bear her cold, silent composure. Revulsion overcame him when he even thought of her—her croaking voice, her greasy hair, her dull, animal, merciless absence of feeling, and part of his anger was anger against himself because he lacked the power to break the bond between them by force, like a piece of string, although it was almost throttling him. So he saw only one way out—flight. He packed his case in secret without a word to her, leaving only a hasty note behind to say that he had gone to visit friends in Carinthia.

The Baron stayed away all summer. Returning once during that time, when he was called back to Vienna on urgent business concerning his late wife's estate, he preferred to come quietly, stay in a hotel, and send no word to that bird of ill omen waiting for him at home. Crescenz never learned of his presence because she spoke to no one. With nothing to do, dark-faced, she sat in the kitchen all day, went to church twice instead of once a week as before, received instructions and money to settle bills from the Baron's lawyer, but she heard nothing from the Baron himself. He did not write and he sent her no messages. She sat there silently, waiting: her face became harder and thinner, her movements were wooden again, and so she spent many weeks, waiting and waiting in a mysterious state of rigidity.

In autumn, however, urgent business no longer allowed the Baron to extend his stay in the country, and he had to return to his apartment. At the doorway of the building he stopped, hesitating. Two months in the company of close friends had almost made him forget a good deal of it—but now that he was about to confront his nightmare again in physical form, the person who perhaps was his accomplice, he felt exactly the same nauseating spasm as before. It made him retch. With every step he took as he went more and more slowly up the stairs, that invisible hand crept up his throat and tightened its grip. In the end he had to make a mighty effort to summon up all his will-power and force his stiff fingers to turn the key in the lock.

Surprised, Crescenz came out of the kitchen as soon as she heard the click of the key turning. When she saw him, she stood there looking pale for a moment, and then, as if ducking out of sight, bent to pick up the travelling bag he had put down. But she said not a word of greeting, and he said nothing either. In silence she carried the bag to his room; he followed in silence too. He waited in silence, looking out of the window, until she had left the room. Then he hastily turned the key in the door.

That was their first meeting after several months.

Crescenz waited. And so did the Baron, to see if that dreadful spasm of horror at the sight of her would pass off. It did not. Even before he saw her, the mere sound of her footsteps in the corridor outside his room sent the sense of discomfort fluttering up in him. He did not touch his breakfast, he was quick to leave the house every morning without a word to her, and he stayed out until late at night merely to avoid her presence. He delivered the two or three instructions that he had to give her with his face averted. It choked him to breathe the air of the same room as this spectral creature.

Meanwhile, Crescenz sat silently on her wooden stool all day. She was not cooking anything for herself. She couldn't stomach food, she avoided all human company, she just sat with timidity in her eyes, waiting for the first whistle from her master, like a beaten dog which knows that it has done something bad. Her dull mind did not understand exactly what had happened, only that her lord and master was avoiding her and didn't want her any more. That was all that reached her, and it made a powerful impression.

On the third day after the Baron's return the doorbell rang. A composed, grey-haired man with a clean-shaven face was standing there with a suitcase in his hand. Crescenz was about to send him away, but the intruder insisted that he was the new manservant here, his master had asked him to arrive at ten, and she was to announce him. Crescenz went white as a sheet; she stood there for a moment with her stiff fingers spread wide in mid-air. Then her hand fell like a bird that has been shot. "Thassa way," she abruptly told the surprised man, turned to the kitchen and slammed the door behind her.

The manservant stayed. From that day on her master no longer had to say a word to her; all messages were relayed by the calm, elderly servant. She did not know what was going on in the apartment; it all flowed over her like a cold wave flowing over a stone.

This oppressive state of affairs lasted for two weeks, draining Crescenz like an illness. Her face was thin and haggard, the hair was suddenly going grey at her temples. Her movements froze entirely. She spent almost all the time sitting on her wooden stool, like a block of wood herself, staring blankly at the empty window, and if she did work she worked furiously, like someone in a violent outbreak of rage.

After those two weeks the manservant went to his master's room, and from his tactful air of biding his time the Baron realised that there was something he particularly wanted to say. The man had already complained of the sullen manner of that 'Tyrolean clod', as he contemptuously called her, and had suggested dismissing her. But feeling in some way painfully embarrassed, the Baron had initially pretended to ignore his proposal. Although at the time the servant had bowed and left the room, this time he stuck doggedly to his opinion, and with a strange, almost awkward expression he finally stammered that he hoped sir would not think he was being ridiculous, but he couldn't ... no, he couldn't put it any other way ... he was *afraid* of her. That surly, withdrawn creature was unbearable, he didn't think the Baron knew what a dangerous person he had in his home.

The Baron instinctively started at this warning. What did the man mean, he asked, what was he trying to say? The manservant did soften his statement by saying that he couldn't point to anything certain, he just had a feeling that the woman was like a rabid animal … she could easily do someone harm. Yesterday he turned to give her an order, and he had unexpectedly seen a look in her eyes—well, there wasn't much you could say about a look, but it had been as if she was about to spring at his throat. And since then he had been afraid of her—even afraid to touch the food she cooked. "You wouldn't have any idea, sir," he concluded, "what a dangerous person that is. She don't speak, she don't say much, but I think she's capable of murder." Startled, the Baron cast the man a quick glance. Had he heard anything definite? Had someone passed any suspicion on to him? He felt his fingers begin to shake, and hastily put his cigar down so that the trembling of his hands would not show. But the elderly man's face was entirely unsuspecting—no, he couldn't know anything. The Baron hesitated. Then he suddenly pulled himself together, knowing what he himself wanted to do, and made up his mind. "Well, wait a little while, but if she's so unfriendly to you again then I'll just give her notice."

The manservant bowed, and the Baron sat back in relief. Every thought of that mysteriously dangerous creature darkened the day for him. It would be best to do it while he was away, he thought, at Christmas, per- haps—the mere idea of the liberation he hoped for did him good. Yes, that will be best, he told himself once more, at Christmas when I'm away.

But the very next day, as soon as he had gone to his study after dinner, there was a knock at the door. Unthinkingly looking up from his newspaper, he murmured, "Come in." And then he heard that dreaded, hard tread that was always in his dreams. He started up: like a death's head, pale and white as chalk, he saw the angular face quivering above the thin black figure. A little pity mingled with his horror when he saw how the anxious footsteps of the creature, crushed as she looked, humbly stopped short at the edge of the carpet. And to hide his bemused state, he tried to sound carefree. "Well, what is it then, Crescenz?" he asked. But it didn't come out warm and jovial, as he had intended; against his own will the question sounded hostile and unpleasant.

Crescenz did not move. She stared at the carpet. At last, as you might push a hard object away with your foot, she managed to get the words out. "That servant, sir, he come ter see 'un. He say sir be going to fire 'un."

The Baron, painfully embarrassed, rose to his feet. He had not expected it to come so soon. He began to say, stammering, that he was sure it hadn't been meant like that, she ought to try to get on with his other servant, adding whatever other unthinking remarks came to his lips.

But Crescenz stayed put, her gaze boring into the carpet, her shoulders hunched. Bitter and dogged, she kept her head bowed like an ox, letting all his kindly remarks pass her by, waiting for just one word that did not come. And when at last he fell silent, exhausted and rather repelled by the contemptible role he was obliged to adopt, trying to ingratiate himself with a servant, she remained obstinate and mute. Then at last she got out something else. "I only wants ter know if sir himself tells Anton ter fire 'un."

She somehow got it out—harshly, reluctantly, violently. And already on edge as he was, he felt it like a blow. Was that a threat? Was she challenging him? All at once all his cowardice was gone, and all his pity. The hatred and disgust that had been dammed up in him for weeks came together with his ardent wish to make an end of it at last. And suddenly changing his tone entirely, and adopting the cool objectivity that he had learned at work in the ministry, he confirmed, as if it were of no importance, that yes, that was indeed so, he had in fact given the manservant a free hand to organise the household just as he liked. He personally wished her well, and would try to persuade Anton to change his mind about dismissing her. But if she still insisted on maintaining hostilities with the manservant, well, he would just have to dispense with her services.

And summoning up all his will-power, determined not to be deterred by any sly hint or insinuating remark, he turned his glance as he spoke these last words on the woman he assumed to be threatening him and looked straight at her.

But the eyes that Crescenz now raised timidly from the floor were those of a wounded animal, seeing the pack just about to break out of the bushes ahead of her. "Th ... thank 'ee, sir" she got out, very faintly. "I be goin' ... I won't trouble sir no more ... "

And slowly, without turning, she dragged herself out of the door with her bowed shoulders and stiff, wooden footsteps.

That evening, when the Baron came back from the opera and reached for the letters that had arrived on his desk, he saw something strange and rectangular there. As the light flared up, he made out a wooden casket with rustic carving. It was not locked: inside, neatly arranged, lay all the little things that he had ever given Crescenz: a few cards from his hunting expeditions, two theatre tickets, a silver ring, the entire heaped rectangle of her banknotes, and there was also a snapshot taken twenty years ago in the Tyrol in which her eyes, obviously taken unawares by the flashlight, stared out with the same stricken, beaten look as they had a few hours ago when she left his study.

At something of a loss, the Baron pushed the casket aside and went out to ask the manservant what these things of Crescenz's were doing on his desk. The servant immediately offered to bring his enemy in to account for herself. But Crescenz was not to be found in the kitchen or anywhere else in the apartment. And only the next day, when the police reported the suicidal fall of a woman about forty years old from the bridge over the Danube Canal, did the two men know the answer to the question of where Leporella had gone.

INCIDENT ON LAKE GENEVA

ON THE BANKS OF LAKE GENEVA, close to the small Swiss resort of Villeneuve, a fisherman who had rowed his boat out into the lake one summer night in the year 1918 noticed a strange object in the middle of the water. When he came closer, he saw that it was a raft made of loosely assembled wooden planks which a naked man was clumsily trying to propel forward, using a piece of board as an oar. In astonishment, the fisherman steered his boat that way, helped the exhausted man into it, used some fishing nets as a makeshift covering for his nakedness, and then tried questioning the shivering figure huddling nervously into the corner of the boat. But he replied in a strange language, not a word of which was anything like the fisherman's, so the rescuer soon gave up any further attempts, pulled in his nets, and rowed back to the bank, plying his oars faster than before.

As the early light of dawn showed the outline of the bank, the naked man's face too began to clear. A child-like smile appeared through the tangled beard around his broad mouth, he raised one hand, pointing, and kept stammering out a single word over and over again: a question that was half a statement. It sounded like "*Rossiya*", and he repeated it more and more happily the closer the keel came to the bank of the lake. At last the boat crunched on the beach; the fisherman's womenfolk, who were waiting for him to land his dripping catch, scattered screeching, like Nausicaa's maids in the days of

131

old, when they caught sight of the naked man covered by fishing nets, and only gradually, on hearing the strange news, did several men from the village appear. They were soon joined by that local worthy the courthouse usher, eagerly officious and very much on his dignity. He knew at once, from various instructions that he had received and a wealth of wartime experience, that this must be a deserter who had swum over the lake from the French bank, and he was preparing to interrogate him officially, but any such elaborate process was quickly deprived of any dignity or usefulness by the fact that the naked man (to whom some of the locals had now thrown a jacket and a pair of cotton drill trousers) responded to all questions with his questioning cry of *"Rossiya? Rossiya?"* sounding ever more anxious and doubtful. Slightly irked by his failure, the usher ordered the stranger to follow him by means of gestures that could not be misunderstood, and the wet, barefoot figure, his jacket and trousers flapping around him, was escorted to the courthouse, surrounded by the vociferous youths of the village who had now come along, and was taken into custody there. He did not protest, he said not a word, but his bright eyes had darkened with disappointment, and his shoulders were hunched as if expecting blows.

By now news of this human catch had reached the nearby hotel, and several ladies and gentlemen, glad of this intriguing episode to relieve the monotonous course of the day's events, came over to look at the wild man. One lady gave him some confectionery, which he eyed as suspiciously as a monkey might, and did not touch. A gentleman took a photograph. They all chattered and talked vivaciously as they swarmed around him, until at last the manager of the large hotel, who had lived abroad for a long time and knew several languages, spoke to the terrified man first in German, then in Italian and English, and finally in Russian. No sooner did he hear the first sound of his native tongue than the frightened man started violently, a broad smile split his good-natured face from ear to ear, and suddenly he was telling his whole story frankly and with self-assurance. It was very long and very confused, and the chance-come interpreter could not always understand every detail, but in essentials the man's history was as follows:

He had been fighting in Russia, and then one day he and a thousand others were packed into railway trucks and taken a very long way, they were transferred to ships and had travelled in those for even longer, through regions where it was so hot that, as he put it, the bones were baked soft inside your body. Finally they were landed again somewhere or other, packed into more railway trucks, and then they were suddenly told to storm a hill, but he knew no more about that, because a bullet had hit him in the leg as soon as the attack began. The audience, for whom the interpreter translated his questions and the man's answers, immediately realised that this fugitive was a member of one of those Russian divisions fighting in France who had been sent half-way round the world, from Siberia and Vladivostok to the French front, and as well as feeling a certain pity they were all moved at the same time by curiosity: what could have induced him to make this strange attempt at flight? With a smile that was half-good-natured, half-crafty, the Russian readily explained that as soon as he was better he had asked the orderlies where Russia was, and they had pointed to show him the way. He had roughly remembered the direction by noting the position of the sun and the stars, and so he had escaped in secret, walking by night and hiding in haystacks from patrols by day. He had eaten fruit and begged for bread for ten days, until at last he reached this lake. Now his account became less clear. Apparently he himself came from Lake Baikal, and seeing the undulating curves of the opposite bank ahead of him in the evening light, he had thought that Russia must lie over there. At any rate, he had stolen a couple of planks from a hut, and lying face downwards over them, had used a piece of old board as a paddle to make his way far out into the lake, where the fisherman found him. As soon as the hotel manager had translated the anxious question which concluded his confused explanation—could he get home tomorrow?—its naivety at first aroused loud laughter, but that soon turned to pity, and everyone found a few coins or banknotes to give the poor man, who was now looking around him with miserable uncertainty.

By this time a telephone call to Montreux had brought the arrival of a senior police officer to take down an account of the case, rather an arduous task. For not only was the amateur interpreter's command of Russian inadequate, it was soon obvious that the man was uneducated to a degree scarcely comprehensible to Westerners. All he knew about himself was his own first name of Boris, and he was able to give only the most confused accounts of his native village, for instance that the people there were serfs of Prince Metchersky (he used the word serfs although serfdom had been abolished long ago), and that he lived fifty versts from the great lake with his wife and three children. Now a discussion of what was to be done with him began, while he stood amidst the disputants dull-eyed and hunching his shoulders. Some thought he ought to be handed over to the Russian embassy in Berne, others feared that such a measure would get him sent back to France; the police officer explained all the difficulty of deciding whether he should be treated as a deserter or a foreigner without papers; the local court-house usher rejected out of hand any suggestion that the stranger should be fed and accommodated in Villeneuve itself. A Frenchman protested that there was no need to make such a fuss about a miserable runaway; he had better either work or be sent back. Two women objected strongly to this remark, saying that his misfortune wasn't his own fault, and it was a crime to send people away from their homes to a foreign country. It began to look as if this chance incident would lead to political strife when suddenly an old Danish gentleman intervened, saying in firm tones that he would pay for the man's board and lodging for a week, and meanwhile the authorities could come to some agreement with the embassy. This unexpected solution satisfied both the officials and the private parties.

During the increasingly agitated discussion the fugitive's timid gaze had gradually lifted, and his eyes were now fixed on the lips of the hotel manager, the only person in all this turmoil who, he knew, could tell him his fate in terms that he was able to understand. He seemed to be vaguely aware of the turmoil caused by his presence, and as the noisy argument died down he spontaneously raised both hands in the silence, and reached them out to the manager with the pleading look of women at prayer before a holy picture. This moving gesture had an irresistible effect on all present. The manager went up to the man and reassured him warmly, saying that he had nothing to fear, he could stay here and come to no harm, he would have accommodation for the immediate future. The Russian tried to kiss his hand, but the other man withdrew it and quickly stepped back. Then he pointed out the house next door, a small village inn where the Russian would have bed and board, said a few more words of reassurance to him, and then, with another friendly wave, went up the beach to his hotel.

The motionless fugitive stared after him, and as the only person who understood his language dwindled in the distance, his face, which had brightened, grew gloomy again. His avid glances followed the figure of the manager as he went away, going up to the hotel above the bank of the lake, and he took no notice of the others present who were smiling at his strange demeanour. When a sympathetic bystander touched him and pointed to the inn, his heavy shoulders seemed to slump, and he went to the doorway with his head bowed. The bar was opened for him. He sat down at the table, where the barmaid brought him a glass of brandy by way of welcome, and stayed there without moving all afternoon, his eyes clouded. The village children kept looking in at the windows, laughing and shouting something at him—he never raised his head. Customers coming in looked at him curiously, but he sat where he was, back bowed, eyes staring at the table, shy and bashful. And when a crowd of guests came in to eat at midday and filled the room with their laughter, while hundreds of words he did not understand swirled around him and he himself, horribly aware of being a foreigner here, sat deaf and mute amidst the general liveliness, his hands trembled so badly that he could hardly raise the spoon from his soup. Suddenly a large tear ran down his cheek and dropped heavily on the table. He looked timidly around him. The others present had noticed the tear, and suddenly fell silent. And he felt ashamed; his large, shaggy head sank closer and closer to the black wood of the table.

He sat like that until evening. People came and went; he did not notice them, and they had stopped noticing him. He sat in the shadow of the stove like a shadow himself, his hands resting heavily on the table. He was forgotten, and no one saw him suddenly rise when twilight came and go up the path to the hotel, plodding lethargically like an animal. He stood for an hour at the door there, cap humbly in his hand, and then for another hour, not looking at anyone. At last this strange figure, standing still and black as a tree stump outside the sparkling lights of the hotel entrance as if he had put down roots there, attracted the attention of one of the pageboys, who fetched the manager. Once again his dark face lightened a little when he heard his own language.

"What do you want, Boris?" asked the manager kindly.

"Forgive me," stammered the fugitive, "I only wanted … I wanted to know if I can go home."

"Of course, Boris, to be sure you can go home," smiled the manager.

"Tomorrow?"

Now the other man looked grave too. The words had been spoken in so pleading a tone that the smile vanished from his face.

"No, Boris … not just yet. Not until the war is over."

"When is that? When will the war be over?"

"God only knows. We humans don't."

"But before that? Can't I go before that?"

"No, Boris."

"Is it so far to go?"

"Yes."

"Many more days' journey?"

"Many more days."

"I'll go all the same, sir. I'm strong. I don't tire easily."

"But you can't, Boris. There's a border between here and your home."

"A border?" He looked blank. The word was new to him. Then he said again, with his extraordinary obstinacy, "I'll swim over it."

The manager almost smiled. But he was painfully moved, and explained gently, "No, Boris, that's impossible. A border means there's a foreign country on the other side. People won't let you through."

"But I won't hurt them! I threw my rifle away. Why wouldn't they let me go back to my wife, if I ask them in Christ's name?"

The manager was feeling increasingly heavy at heart. Bitterness rose in him. "No," he said, "they won't let you through, Boris. People don't take any notice of the word of Christ any more."

"But what am I to do, sir? I can't stay here! The people

that live here don't understand me, and I don't understand them."

"You'll soon learn, Boris."

"No, sir." The Russian bowed his head. "I can't learn things. I can only work in the fields, that's all I know how to do. What would I do here? I want to go home! Show me the way!"

"There isn't any way at the moment, Boris."

"But sir, they can't forbid me to go home to my wife and my children! I'm not a soldier any more."

"Oh yes, they can, Boris."

"What about the Tsar?" He asked the question very suddenly, trembling with expectation and awe.

"There's no Tsar any more, Boris. He's been deposed."

"No Tsar any more?" He stared dully at the other man, the last glimmer of light went out in his eyes, and then he said very wearily, "So I can't go home?"

"Not yet. You'll have to wait, Boris."

The face in the dark grew ever gloomier. "I've waited so long already! I can't wait any more. Show me the way to go! I want to try!"

"There's no way, Boris. They'd arrest you at the border. Stay here and we'll find you work."

"People here don't understand me, and I don't understand them," he obstinately repeated. "I can't live here! Help me, sir!"

"I can't, Boris."

"Help me, sir, for the sake of Christ! Help me, I can't bear it any more!"

"I can't, Boris. There's no way anyone can help anyone else these days."

They faced each other in silence. Boris was twisting his cap in his hands. "Then why did they take me away from home? They said I had to fight for Russia and the Tsar. But Russia is far away from here, and the Tsar ... what do you say they did to the Tsar?"

"They deposed him."

"Deposed." He repeated the word without understanding it. "What am I to do, sir? I have to go home! My children are crying for me. I can't live here. Help me, sir, help me!"

"I just can't, Boris."

"Can no one help me?"

"Not at the moment."

The Russian bent his head even further, and then said abruptly, in hollow tones, "Thank you, sir," and turned away.

He went down the path very slowly. The hotel manager watched him for a long time, and was surprised when he did not go to the inn, but on down the steps to the lake. He sighed deeply and went back to his work in the hotel.

As chance would have it, it was the same fisherman who found the drowned man's naked body next morning. He had carefully placed the trousers, cap and jacket that he had been given on the bank, and went into the water just as he had come out of it. A statement was taken about the incident, and since no one knew the stranger's full name, a cheap wooden cross was put on the place where he was buried, one of those little crosses planted over the graves of unknown soldiers that now cover the continent of Europe from end to end.

TRANSLATOR'S
AFTERWORD

IN THEIR VARIOUS WAYS the four stories by Stefan Zweig in this volume, two long and two quite short, could all be regarded as studies in suicide. The events leading to the deaths of the four central characters however, are very different. The narrator of *Amok*, a doctor in the grip of sexual obsession and guilt, ultimately drowns himself in the Bay of Naples in order to protect the guilty secret of an extra-marital pregnancy followed by a botched back-street abortion. His tragic tale, told to a chance-met shipboard companion, employs Zweig's favourite device of a central story within a framework narrative, imparting a touch of the Ancient Mariner to the doctor's compulsive monologue, which with its early twentieth-century colonial setting has also dark Conradian complexities.

The suicide of the central character of *Leporella*, the slow-witted maidservant Crescenz whose absolute devotion to her employer leads her to murder his unloved wife, is the climax of a chilling murder story. Once her services are rejected by the Baron for whom she did anything and everything she could—and who is horrified to discover just what she has done—life leads nowhere but to the water of the Danube Canal in Vienna. And the two shorter stories also end in suicide: François, the waiter from the Grand Hotel in *The Star above the Forest* who has fallen hopelessly in love with an aristocratic hotel guest, cannot bear to lose even the sight of her for ever, and finds a final union only by letting the wheels of the train carrying her away crush him as he lies on the tracks. In *Incident on Lake Geneva*, a First World War Russian prisoner-of-war, who has made his way to the banks of the Swiss lake believing that his native land lies only on the other side of the water is cast into such despair on learning how unattainable return from exile still is that he drowns himself, giving up all hope of ever being reunited with his wife and children.

One might reasonably suppose, then, that Stefan Zweig, like Webster in T S Eliot's famous line, was much possessed by death. Yet although the elegiac note prevails, in all these four suicides there are gleams of light, certain redeeming features. For example, even in the character of the maid-servant Crescenz, nicknamed by her employer's mistress Leporella after the manservant Leporello in *Don Giovanni*. There is pathos in her story, and her premeditated murder of the Baroness is committed as much from a twisted idea of duty and devotion as out of sheer malice, although malice also enters the equation. The doctor narrator of *Amok* finds a kind of absolution in going to his death with the body of the woman he had loved, in order to fulfil her dying wish and save her reputation. The protagonists of the shorter stories both die literally for love, in despair at being parted from the objects of their desire. Their suicides are almost wished for; the waiter François suffers an almost lyrical death, a *Liebestod* accepted with peaceful resignation, which somehow momentarily and almost mystically stirs the heart of the woman who knew him only as a member of the hotel staff. And ironically, the first line of *Incident on Lake Geneva*, giving the date of the story as 1918, makes it clear that perhaps it would not have been so long before the Russian prisoner-of-war was able to make his way home after all.

Ironically too, when Stefan Zweig and his second wife themselves committed suicide in 1942, it seems to have been in despair at the turn that the Second World War appeared to be taking. Zweig had already been appalled by the horrors of the 1914-1918 war; between the wars, as an Austrian Jew, he had been obliged to go into exile abroad when Nazi anti-Semitism threatened anyone of Jewish descent, whether they were a practising Jew or not. In forcing so many fine writers, artists and musicians to leave, Germany and Austria, nations that took such well-justified pride in their artistic culture, wilfully deprived themselves of many who had made a huge contribution to it, and would continue to create fine works in exile. Zweig went first to live in England, then to the United States, and finally moved to Brazil. In February 1942 the fall of Singapore, one of the worst British defeats suffered in the war, made it seem to him that the Nazis and their Japanese allies were on the point of conquering the world, and a few days later he and his wife killed themselves.

In yet another twist of irony, one that has been noted by many readers and literary critics, the last novella that Zweig wrote, *Schachnovelle* (*The Royal Game*), has as its protagonist a man who successfully withstands psychological torture by the Nazis through sheer force of mind. He emerges frail and damaged from his ordeal, but he survives. The fact that Zweig did not is yet another indictment of the Nazi regime that turned its back on all the civilising influences of the pan-European culture in which he was so much at home. He was not gassed in a death camp, but Hitler, with whose intentions he had become obsessed, can be said to have killed him just the same, when another twenty years of life and creative work might still have lain ahead of him.